For a split second Thorne imagined a mite of a woman with wide gold eyes and a fleeting smile at his side.

He pulled himself up short. What was he thinking? Nicole was his sister's physician and that was it. Nothing more. Yet, ever since he'd first seen her in her office at the hospital, he hadn't been able to force her from his mind. It hadn't helped that when he'd caught up with her in the parking lot, he'd seen her not as Randi's doctor, but as a woman—a beautiful, bright and articulate woman. He hadn't been able to stop himself from kissing her and he'd been thinking about it off and on ever since. Nicole Sanders Stevenson was all grown up, educated and self-confident—more intriguing now than she had been as a girl of seventeen. Despite her small stature, she was a force to be reckoned with—way too much trouble for any man.

And yet...

Dear Reader,

The most wonderful time of the year just got better! These six captivating romances from Special Edition are sure to brighten your holidays.

Reader favorite Sherryl Woods is back by popular demand with the latest addition to her series AND BABY MAKES THREE: THE DELACOURTS OF TEXAS. In *The Delacourt Scandal,* a curious reporter seeking revenge unexpectedly finds love.

And just in time for the holidays, Lisa Jackson kicks off her exciting new miniseries THE McCAFFERTYS with *The McCaffertys: Thorne,* where a hero's investigation takes an interesting turn when he finds himself face-to-face with his ex-lover. Unwrap the next book in A RANCHING FAMILY, a special gift this month from Victoria Pade. In *The Cowboy's Gift-Wrapped Bride,* a Wyoming rancher is startled not only by his undeniable attraction to an amnesiac beauty he found in a blizzard, but also by the tantalizing secrets she reveals as she regains her memory.

And in RUMOR HAS IT…, a couple separated by tragedy in the past finally has a chance for love in Penny Richards's compelling romance, *Lara's Lover.* The holiday cheer continues with Allison Leigh's emotional tale of a runaway American heiress who becomes a *Mother in a Moment* after she agrees to be nanny to a passel of tots.

And silver wedding bells are ringing as Nikki Benjamin wraps up the HERE COME THE BRIDES series with the heartwarming story of a hometown hero who convinces his childhood sweetheart to become his *Expectant Bride-To-Be.*

I hope all of these breathtaking romances warm your hearts and add joy to your holiday season.

Best,
Karen Taylor Richman
Senior Editor

Please address questions and book requests to:
Silhouette Reader Service
U.S.: 3010 Walden Ave., P.O. Box 1325, Buffalo, NY 14269
Canadian: P.O. Box 609, Fort Erie, Ont. L2A 5X3

The McCaffertys: Thorne

LISA JACKSON

SPECIAL EDITION™

Published by Silhouette Books

America's Publisher of Contemporary Romance

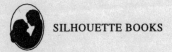 SILHOUETTE BOOKS

ISBN 0-373-24364-2

THE McCAFFERTYS: THORNE

Copyright © 2000 by Susan Crose

Visit Silhouette at www.eHarlequin.com

Printed in U.S.A.

Books by Lisa Jackson

Silhouette Special Edition

A Twist of Fate #118
The Shadow of Time #180
Tears of Pride #194
Pirate's Gold #215
A Dangerous Precedent #233
Innocent by Association #244
Midnight Sun #264
Devil's Gambit #282
Zachary's Law #296
Yesterday's Lies #315
One Man's Love #358
Renegade Son #376
Snowbound #394
Summer Rain #419
Hurricane Force #467
In Honor's Shadow #495
Aftermath #525
Tender Trap #569
With No Regrets #611
Double Exposure #636
Mystery Man #653
Obsession #691
Sail Away #720
Million Dollar Baby #743
*He's a Bad Boy #787
*He's Just a Cowboy #799
*He's the Rich Boy #811
A Husband To Remember #835
*He's My Soldier Boy #866
†A Is for Always #914
†B Is for Baby #920
†C Is for Cowboy #926
†D Is for Dani's Baby #985
New Year's Daddy #1004
‡A Family Kind of Guy #1191
‡A Family Kind of Gal #1207
‡A Family Kind of Wedding #1219
§The McCaffertys: Thorne #1364

Silhouette Intimate Moments

Dark Side of the Moon #39
Gypsy Wind #79
Mystic #158

Silhouette Romance

His Bride To Be #717

Silhouette Books

Silhouette Christmas Stories 1993
"The Man from Pine Mountain"

Fortune's Children
The Millionaire and the Cowgirl

Montana Mavericks: Wed in Whitehorn
Lone Stallion's Lady

*Mavericks
†Love Letters
‡Forever Family
§The McCaffertys

LISA JACKSON

has been writing romances for over ten years. With forty-five Silhouette novels to her credit, she divides her time between writing on the computer, researching her next novel, keeping in touch with her college-age sons and playing tennis. Many of the fictitious small towns in her books resemble Molalla, Oregon, a small logging community, where she and her sister, Silhouette author Natalie Bishop, grew up.

THE McCAFFERTYS

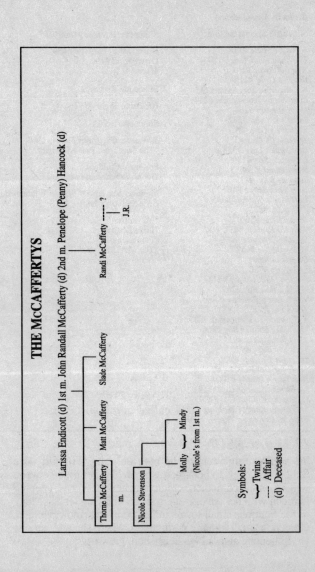

Larissa Endicott (d) 1st m. John Randall McCafferty (d) 2nd m. Penelope (Penny) Hancock (d)

Thorne McCafferty   Matt McCafferty   Slade McCafferty   Randi McCafferty ---- ?

m.   Nicole Stevenson

Molly   Mindy
(Nicole's from 1st m.)

J.R.

Symbols:
⁓ Twins
--- Affair
(d) Deceased

Prologue

Last Summer

"The truth of the matter, son, is that I've got a request for you," John Randall McCafferty stated from his wheelchair. He'd asked Thorne to push him to the fence line some thirty yards from the front door of the ranch house he'd called home all his life.

"I hate to ask what it is," Thorne remarked.

"It's simple. I want you to marry. You're thirty-nine, son, Matt's thirty-seven and Slade—well, he's still a boy but he is thirty-six. None of you has married and I don't have one grandchild—well at least none that I know of." He frowned. "Even your sister hasn't settled down."

"Randi's only twenty-six."

"High time," J. Randall said. A shell of the man he'd once been, J. Randall nonetheless gripped the arms of his metal chair, often referred to as "that damned contraption," so tightly his knuckles bleached white. An old afghan was draped over his legs though the temperature hovered near eighty according to the ancient thermometer tacked to the north side of the barn. Across his lap was his cane, another hated symbol of his failing health.

"I'm serious, son. I need to know that the McCafferty line won't die with you boys."

"That's an archaic way of thinking." Thorne wasn't going to be pushed around. Not by his old man. Not by anyone.

"So be it. Damn it, Thorne, if ya haven't noticed I don't have a helluva lot of time left on this here earth!" J. Randall swept his cane from his lap and jabbed it into the ground for emphasis.

Harold, J. Randall's crippled hunting dog, gave off a disgruntled woof from the front porch and a field mouse scurried into a tangle of brambles.

"I don't understand you," J. Randall grumbled. "This could have been yours, boy. All yours." He swept his cane in a wide arc and Thorne's gaze followed his father's gesture. Spindly legged colts frolicked in one pasture while a herd of mottled cattle in shades of russet, black and brown ambled near the dry creek bed that sliced through what was commonly referred to as "the big meadow." The paint on the barn had peeled, the windows in the stables needed replacing and the whole damned place looked as if it were suffering from the same debilitating disease as its owner.

The Flying M Ranch.

John Randall McCafferty's pride and joy. Now run by a foreman as he was too ill and his children too busy with their own lives.

Thorne regarded the rolling acres with a mixture of emotions running the gauntlet from love to hate.

"I'm not getting married, Dad. Not for a while."

"What's the wait? And don't tell me you need to make your mark. You've done it, boy." Old, faded blue eyes rolled up to look at him, then blinked when rays from a blinding Montana sun were too much. "What're ya worth now? Three million? Five?"

"Somewhere around seven."

His father snorted. "I was a rich man once. What did it get me?" His old lips folded back on themselves. "Two wives who bled me dry when we divorced and a bellyful of worry about losin' it all. No, money isn't what counts, Thorne. It's children. And land. Damn it all—" biting his lower lip, J. Randall dug deep into his pocket "—now where in tarnation is that— Oh, here we go."

Slowly he withdrew a ring that winked in the sunlight and Thorne's gut twisted as he recognized the band—his father's first wedding ring; one he hadn't worn in over a quarter of a century. "I want you to have this," the old man said as he held out the gold band with its unique silver inlay. "Your mother gave it to me the day we were married."

"I know." Thorne, sensing he was making a serious mistake, accepted the ring. It felt cold and hard in his fingers, a metal circle that held no warmth, no promise, no joy. A symbol of broken dreams. He pocketed the damn ring.

"Promise me, boy."

"What?"

"That you'll marry."

Thorne didn't bat an eye. "Someday."

"Make it soon, will ya? I'd like to leave this earth knowin' that you were gonna have a family."

"I'll think about it," Thorne said and suddenly the small band of gold and silver in his pocket seemed to weigh a thousand pounds.

Chapter One

Dr. Nicole Stevenson felt a rush of adrenaline surge through her blood as it did each time accident victims were rushed into the emergency room of St. James Hospital.

She met the intensity in Dr. Maureen Oliverio's eyes as the other woman hung up the phone. ''The copter's here! Let's go, people!'' The hastily grouped team of doctors and nurses responded. ''The paramedics are bringing in the patient. You're on, Dr. Stevenson.''

''What have we got?'' Nicole asked.

Dr. Oliverio, a no-nonsense doctor, led the way

through double doors. "Single-car accident up in Glacier Park, the patient's a woman in her late twenties, pregnant, at term. Fractures, internal damage, concussed, a real mess. Membranes have ruptured. We'll probably need to do a C-section because of her other injuries. While we're inside, we'll repair any other damage. Everybody with me? Dr. Stevenson's in charge until we send the patient to OR."

Nicole caught the glances of the other doctors as they adjusted masks and gloves. It was her job to stabilize the patient before shipping her off to surgery.

The doors of the room flew open and a gurney, propelled by two paramedics flew through the doors of the emergency room of St. James Hospital.

"What have we got here?" Nicole asked the nearest paramedic, a short red-faced man with clipped graying hair and a moustache. "What are her vital signs? What about the baby?"

"BP, normal, one-ten over seventy-five, heart rate sixty-two but dropping slightly…" The paramedic rattled off the information he'd gathered and Nicole, listening, looked down at the patient, an unconscious woman whose face once probably beautiful was now bloody and already beginning to bruise. Her abdomen was distended, fluid from an IV flowed into her arm and her neck and head were braced. "…lacerations, abrasions, fractured skull, mandible and femur, possible internal bleeding…"

"Let's get a fetal monitor here!" Nicole ordered as a nurse peeled off.

"On its way."

"Good." Nicole nodded. "Okay, okay, now, let's stabilize the mother."

"Has the husband been notified? Do we have a consent?" Dr. Oliverio asked.

"Don't know," a grim-faced paramedic replied. "The police are trying to locate her relatives. According to her ID, her name is Randi McCafferty and there's no indication of any allergies to meds on her driver's licence, no prescription drugs in her purse."

Oh, God! Nicole's heart nearly stopped. She froze. For a split second her concentration lapsed and she gave herself a quick mental shake. "Are you sure?" she asked the shorter of the two paramedics.

"Positive."

"Randi McCafferty," Dr. Oliverio repeated, sucking in her breath. "My daughter went to school with her. Her father's dead—J. Randall, important man around these parts at one time. Owned the Flying M Ranch about twenty miles out of town. Randi, here, has three half brothers."

And Thorne's one of them, Nicole thought, her jaw tensing.

"What about the husband or boyfriend? The kid's got a father somewhere," Dr. Oliverio insisted.

"Don't know. Never heard of one."

"We'll figure out all that later," Nicole said, taking charge once more. "Right now, let's just concentrate on stabilizing her and the baby."

Dr. Oliverio nodded. "Let's get that fetal monitor on here! STAT."

"Got it," a nurse replied.

"BP's falling, doctor—one hundred over sixty," a nurse said.

"Damn." Nicole's own heart began to pound. She wasn't going to lose this patient. *Come on Randi,* she silently urged. *Where's that good ol' McCafferty fight? Come on, come on!* "Where's the anesthesiologist?" Nicole demanded.

"On his way."

"Who is he?"

"Brummel." Dr. Oliverio met Nicole's gaze. "A good man. He'll be here."

"The monitor's in place," a nurse said just as Dr. Brummel, a thin man in rimless glasses, pushed his way through the doors. "What have we got here?" he asked as he quickly scanned the patient.

"Woman. Unconscious. About to deliver. Single-car accident. No known allergies, no medical records, but we're checking," Nicole said. "She's got a skull fracture, multiple other fractures, pneumothorax—so she's already entubated. Her membranes have ruptured, the kid's on his way, and there might be more abdominal injuries."

"The mother's BP is stabilizing—one hundred and five over sixty," a nurse called, but Nicole didn't relax. Couldn't. In her estimation Randi McCafferty's life wasn't yet certain.

"Keep your eye on it. Now, what about the baby?" Nicole asked.

"We've got trouble here. The baby's in distress," Dr. Oliverio said, eyeing the readout of the fetal monitor.

"Then let's get it out of there."

"I'll be ready in a minute," Dr. Brummel said from behind his mask as he adjusted the breathing tube. Satisfied, he glanced up at Nicole. "Let's go."

"We've got a neonatalogist standing by."

"Good." Nicole checked Randi's vital signs one

last time. "Patient's stable." She glanced at the team, then met Dr. Oliverio's eyes with her own. Randi McCafferty was in an uphill battle for her life. As was the baby. "All right, doctors, the patients are all yours."

Thorne drove like a madman. He'd gotten the call from Slade less than three hours earlier that Randi was in a car accident in Glacier Park, here in Montana.

Thorne had been in Denver at the time, in a private business meeting at the offices of McCafferty International and he'd left abruptly. He told his secretary to handle everything and rearrange his schedule, then he grabbed a duffel bag he kept packed in a closet and had driven to the airfield. Within the hour he was airborne, flying the company jet directly to a private airstrip at the ranch. He hadn't bothered checking with his brothers again, instead he'd just taken the keys to a pickup that was waiting for him, tossed his duffel bag into the truck then taken off for Grand Hope and St. James Hospital where Randi was battling for her life.

He stepped on the accelerator, took a corner too fast and heard the tires squeal in protest. He didn't know what was going on; the phone call from his brother Slade had been broken up by static and eventually disconnected as cell service wasn't the greatest here. But he did understand that Randi's life was in question and that the name of the admitting doctor was Stevenson. Other than that, he knew nothing.

Night-darkened fields flew by. The wipers slapped sleet from the windshield and Thorne's jaw grew hard. What the devil had happened? Why was Randi in Montana when her job was in Seattle? What had she been doing in Glacier Park, how serious were her injuries—was she really in danger of losing her life? A piece of information that finally pierced his brain from his conversation with Slade burrowed deep in his brain. Hadn't his brother said something about Randi being pregnant? No way. He'd seen her less than six months ago. She was single, didn't even have a steady boyfriend. Or did she? What did he really know about his half sister?

Not a helluva lot.

Guilt ripped through him. *You should have kept in contact. You're the oldest. It was your responsibility. It wasn't her fault that her mother seduced your father over a quarter of a century before and broke up John Randall's first marriage. It wasn't her fault that you were just too damned busy with your own life.*

Dozens of questions burned through his conscience as he saw the lights of the town glowing in the distance.

He'd have his answers soon enough.

If Randi survived. His fingers clenched around the wheel and he found himself praying to a God he'd thought had long ago turned a deaf ear.

Thorne McCafferty.

The last person on earth Nicole wanted to deal with. But, no doubt, he'd be here. And soon. As she tore off her surgical gloves, she told herself to buck up. He was just another worried relative of a patient. Nothing more.

Nonetheless Nicole didn't like the idea of facing

him again. There were too many old wounds, too much pain she'd never really resolved, too many emotions that she'd locked away years ago. She'd realized when she moved here after her divorce that she wouldn't be able to avoid Thorne forever. Grand Hope, despite its recent growth, was still a small town and John Randall McCafferty had been one of its leading citizens. His sons and daughter had grown up here.

So she'd have to face Thorne again. Big deal. It was only a matter of time. Unfortunately the situation—with his sister struggling for her life—wasn't the best of circumstances.

Nicole stuffed her stethoscope into her pocket and braced herself. Not only would she have to face Thorne again, but Randi McCafferty's other distraught brothers as well—men she'd known in a lifetime long, long ago when she'd dated their older brother. Her time with Thorne had been short, though. Intense and unforgettable, but thankfully short. His younger brothers, who had been caught up in their own lives at the time, might not remember her.

Don't believe it for a minute. When it comes to women, the McCafferty men were almost legendary in their conquests. They'd known all the girls in town.

Another painful old scar ripped open because Nicole had come to face the fact that she had been nothing more than another one of Thorne McCafferty's conquests, just another notch in his belt. A poor, shy, studious girl who had, for a short period one summer, caught his eye.

An archaic way of thinking, but oh, so torturously true.

Through a high window she saw the movement of stormy gray clouds that reflected her own gloomy thoughts. Though it was only October the weather service had been predicting snow.

She'd been in the ER all day, had nearly finished her shift when Randi McCafferty had been brought in.

Nicole's feet ached, her head pounded and the thought of a shower was pure heaven—a shower, a glass of chilled Chardonnay, a crackling fire and the twins cuddled with her under the quilt in her favorite rocker as she read them a bedtime story. She couldn't help but smile. "Later," she reminded herself. First she had serious business to attend to.

Randi, still in recovery, wasn't out of the woods yet, nor would she be for a while. Comatose and fighting for her life, Randi would spend the better part of the next week in ICU being monitored, her vital signs watched twenty-four hours.

The good news was that the baby, a robust boy, had survived the accident and a quick Cesarean birth. So far.

Sweaty and forcing a smile she didn't feel, Nicole slipped into her lab coat and pushed open the doors to the waiting room where two of Randi McCafferty's brothers sat on chairs, thumbing through magazines, their cups of coffee ignored on a corner table. They were both tall and lanky, handsome men with bold features, expressive eyes and worry written all over their faces.

Looking up as the doors opened, they dropped their magazines and climbed hastily to their feet.

"Mr. McCafferty?" she asked, though she'd spotted them instantly.

"I'm Matt," the taller of the two said as if he didn't recognize her. Maybe that was for the best. Keep the situation as professional as possible. Over six feet, with dark-brown eyes and near-black hair, Matt was dressed in jeans and a Western-cut plaid shirt with the sleeves rolled up. Cowboy boots covered his feet and a stir-stick, chewed flat, was wedged firmly in the corner of his mouth. "This is my brother, Slade."

Again, no hint of recognition lit Slade's gaze. The youngest of the McCafferty brothers, he'd been tagged as the hellion. He was shorter than Matt by less than an inch and a thin scar jagged down one side of a face distinguished by hawkish features and deep-set, startling blue eyes. Wearing a flannel shirt, faded jeans and beat-up tennis shoes, he shifted nervously from one foot to the other.

"I'm Dr. Stevenson, I was on duty when your sister was brought into the ER."

"How's she doin'?" Slade asked anxiously. His eyes narrowed a bit as he looked at her and she realized he'd started the recognition process. It would take a while. It had been years since she'd seen him, her name was different, and there were dozens of women he would have to sift through unless she missed her guess.

She didn't have time for any of that now. Her job was to allay their fears while explaining about Randi's condition. "The surgery went well, but your sister was in pretty rough shape when she was brought in, comatose but in labor. Dr. Oliverio delivered your nephew and he seems healthy, though he'll be given a complete examination by a pediatrician here on staff.

"Randi's prognosis looks good, barring unforeseen complications, but she's survived an incredible trauma." As the brothers listened grimly, Nicole described Randi McCafferty's injuries—concussion, punctured lung, broken ribs, fractured jaw, nearly shattered femur—the list was long and grave. Concern etched in both brothers' features, storm clouds gathering in their eyes. Nicole explained the procedures that had been used to repair the damage, using as many lay terms as possible. Matt's dark skin paled slightly and he winced at one point, looking out the window and chewing the stir-stick until it was thin as parchment. On the other hand, the younger brother, Slade, stared her straight in the face, his jaw clenching, his blue eyes rarely blinking.

As she finished, Slade let out a soft whistle. "Damn it all to hell."

Matt rubbed the stubble on his chin and stared at her. "But she will make it. Right?"

"Unless she takes a turn for the worse, I think so. There's always a question with head injuries, but she's stabilized."

Slade frowned. "She's still in a coma."

"Yes. You understand that I'm the emergency room physician, and other doctors have taken over your sister's care. Each of them will contact you."

"When?" Slade demanded.

"As soon as they can."

She managed a reassuring smile. "I'm going off duty soon. Randi's other doctors will want to talk to you as well. I came out first because I knew you were anxious.'' *And because, damn it, I have a personal connection to your family.*

''Anxious doesn't begin to cover it,'' Matt said and glanced at his watch. ''Shouldn't Thorne be getting here by now?'' he asked his brother.

''He said he was on his way.'' Slade's gaze swung back to Nicole. ''Our oldest brother.'' His eyebrows knit a bit. ''He'll want a full report.''

''No doubt,'' she said and Matt's eyes narrowed. ''I knew him. Years ago.''

She could almost see the wheels turning in the McCafferty brothers' minds, but the situation with their sister was too imminent, too dire, to be distracted.

''But Randi, she's gonna be okay,'' Matt said slowly, doubts shadowing his brown eyes.

''We're hopeful. As I said, she's stabilized, but there's always a question with head injuries.'' Nicole wished she could instill more confidence, allay their worries, but couldn't. ''The truth is, it's gonna be touch-and-go for a while, but she'll be monitored around the clock.''

''Oh, God,'' Slade whispered and the words sounded more like a prayer than a curse.

''I—we appreciate everything you and the other doctors have done.'' Matt shot his brother a look meant to silence him. ''I just want you to know that whatever she needs, specialists, equipment, whatever, we want her to have it.''

''She does,'' Nicole said firmly. In her estimation the staff, facilities and equipment at St. James were

excellent, the best she'd seen in a town the size of
Grand Hope.

"And the baby? You said he's okay, right?" Matt
asked.

"He seems fine, but he's being observed for any
signs of trauma. He's in pediatric ICU, as a precaution
for the next few hours, just to make sure that he's
strong. From all outward appearances, he's healthy
and hale, we're just being doubly cautious especially
since your sister was in labor and her water had broken before she got to the hospital. Dr. Oliverio will
have more details and of course the pediatrician will
get in touch with you as well."

"Damn," Slade whispered while Matt stood silent
and stern.

"When can we see Randi?" Matt asked.

"Soon. She's still in Recovery. Once she's settled
in ICU and her doctors are satisfied with her condition, she can have visitors—just immediate family—
for a few minutes a day. One at a time. Again, her
physician will let you know."

Matt nodded and Slade's fist clenched, but neither
argued. Both brothers' jaws were square and set, the
McCafferty resemblance impossible to ignore.

"You have to understand that Randi's comatose.
She won't respond to you until she wakes up and I
don't know when that will be—oh, here we go. One
of Randi's doctors." Spying Dr. Oliverio walking
down the hallway, Nicole took a few minutes to in-
troduce the McCafferty brothers, then, excusing herself, made her way to her office.

It was a small room with one window. It barely
had enough space for her desk and file cabinet. She

usually transcribed her own notes and after shrugging out of her lab coat, flipped on the computer and spent nearly a half an hour at the keyboard writing a report on Randi McCafferty. As she finished, she reached for the phone. Dialing her home number by rote, she massaged the back of her neck and heard the strains of piped-in music for the first time since she'd walked into the hospital hours before.

"Hello?" Jenny Riley answered on the second ring. Jenny, a student at a local community college, watched Nicole's twins while she worked.

"Hi. It's Nicole. Just wanted to know what was going on. I'll be outta here in about—" she checked her watch and sighed "—probably another hour. Anything I should pick up on the way?"

"How about a ray or two of sunshine for Molly?" Jenny quipped. "She's been in a bad mood ever since she woke up from her nap."

"Has she?" Nicole grinned as she leaned back in her chair so far that it squeaked in protest. Molly, more precocious than her twin sister, was known to wake up grumpy while Mindy, the shier half of the two girls, always smiled, even when rousted from a nap.

"The worst."

"Am not!" a tiny, impertinent voice disagreed.

"Sure you are, but I love you anyway," Jenny said, her voice softer as she turned away from the phone.

"Am not the worst!"

Still grinning, Nicole rested a foot on her desk and sighed. The struggles of the day melted away when she thought of her daughters, two four-year-old dynamos who kept her running, the reasons she'd stayed sane after her divorce.

"Tell them I'll bring home pizza if they're good." She listened as Jenny relayed the message and heard a squeal of delight.

"They're pumped now," Jenny assured her and Nicole laughed just as there was a sharp rap on the door before it was pushed open abruptly. A tall man—maybe six foot three or four—nearly filled the frame. Her heart plummeted as she recognized Thorne.

"Dr. Stevenson?" he demanded, his face set and stern before recognition flared in his eyes and for the briefest of seconds she saw regret chase across his face.

"Look Jenny, I've got to go," she said into the receiver as she hung up slowly, righted her chair and dropped her feet to the floor.

"Nikki?" he said, disbelieving.

Nicole stood but on her side of the desk, her barely five-foot-three-inch frame no match for his height. "Dr. Stevenson now."

"You're Randi's doctor?"

"The ER physician who admitted her." Why, after all the time that had passed and all the pain, did she still feel a ridiculous flutter of disappointment that he hadn't, in all the years since she'd last seen him, ever looked her up? It was silly. Stupid. Beyond naive. And it had no business here; not when his sister was fighting for her life. "I'm not her doctor, you understand. I helped stabilize her for surgery, then the team took over, but I did stop to speak with your brothers out of courtesy because I knew they'd been waiting a long time and the surgeons were still wrapping things up.''

''I see.'' Thorne's handsome face had aged over the years. No longer were any vestiges of boyhood visible. His features were set and stern, matched only by the severity of his black suit, crisp white shirt and tie—the mark of a CEO of his own little empire. ''I didn't know—didn't expect to find you here.''

''I imagine not.''

His eyes, a deep, troubled gray, held hers in a gaze that she knew was often daunting but now seemed weary and worried sick. ''Did you see your brothers in ICU?'' Nicole asked.

''I came directly here. Slade called, said a Dr. Stevenson was in charge, so when I got here, I asked for you at the information desk.'' As if reading the questions in her eyes, he added, ''I wanted to know what I was dealing with before I saw Randi.''

''Fair enough.'' She waved him into the office and motioned to the small plastic chair on the other side of the desk. ''Have a seat. I'll tell you what I know, then you can talk to Randi's other doctors about her prognosis.'' As she reached for her lab coat, she leveled a gaze at him that had been known to shrink even the cockiest of interns. She wanted him to understand. She was no longer the needy little girl he'd dated, seduced and tossed aside. ''But I think we should get something straight right now. As you can see this is my private office. Usually people knock, then wait for an answer, before they come barging in.''

His jaw tightened. ''I was in a hurry. But—fine. Next time I'll remember.''

Oh, Thorne, there's never gonna be a next time.
"Good."

"So she's in ICU?" Thorne asked.

"Yes." Nicole sketched out the details of Randi's emergency arrival to St. James, her conditions and the ensuing procedures. Thorne listened, his expression solemn, his gray eyes never leaving her face.

Once she was finished, he asked a few quick questions, loosened his tie and said, "Let's go."

"To ICU? Both of us?"

"Yes." He was on his feet.

Nicole bristled a bit, ready to fight fire with fire until she spied the hint of pain in his gaze and a twinge of some other emotion that bordered on guilt.

"I suppose I can do that," she agreed, hazarding a glance at her watch. She was running late, but being behind schedule came with the territory. As did dealing with worried relatives of her patients. "Let me make sure she's out of Recovery first." Nicole made a quick phone call, discovered that Randi had been transferred and explained that she and the patient's brother were on their way. For the duration of the short conversation she felt the weight of Thorne McCafferty's gaze upon her and she wondered if he remembered anything about the relationship that had changed the course of her life. Probably not. Once his initial shock at recognizing her had worn off, he was all business. "Okay," she said hanging up. "All set. Matt and Slade have already seen Randi and the nurse on duty wasn't crazy about a third visitor, but I persuaded her."

"Are my brothers still here?"

"I don't know. They told the nurse they'd be back

but didn't say when.'' She adjusted her lab coat and rounded the desk. He had the manners to hold the door for her and as they swept down the hallways he kept up with her fast pace, his long strides equal to two of hers. She'd forgotten that about him. But then she'd tried to erase every memory she'd ever had of him.

A foot taller than she, intimidating and forceful, Thorne walked the same way he faced life—with a purpose. She wondered if he'd ever had a frivolous moment in his life. Years before, she'd realized that even those stolen hours with her had been all a part of Thorne's plan.

At the elevator, Nicole waited as a gurney carrying a frail-looking elderly woman connected to an IV drip was pushed into the hallway by an aide, then she stepped inside. The doors shut. She and Thorne were alone. For the first time in years. He stood ramrod stiff beside her and if he noticed the intimacy of the elevator car, he didn't show it. His face was set, his shoulders square, his gaze riveted to the panel displaying the floor numbers.

Silly as it was, Nicole couldn't remember having ever been so uncomfortable.

The elevator jerked to a stop and as they walked through the carpeted hallways, Thorne finally broke the silence. ''On the telephone, Slade mentioned something about Randi not making it.''

''There's always that chance when injuries are as severe as your sister's.'' They'd reached the doors of the Intensive Care Unit and she, reminding herself to remain professional at all times, angled her head upward to stare straight into his steel-colored eyes. ''But

she's young and strong, getting the best medical care
we can provide, so there's no need to borrow trouble,
or voice your concerns around your sister. She's
comatose, yes, but we don't know what she does or
doesn't hear or feel. Please, for her sake, keep all your
worries and doubts to yourself.'' He seemed about to
protest and by instinct, Nicole reached forward and
touched his hand, her fingers encountering skin that
was hard and surprisingly callused. ''We're doing everything we can, Thorne,'' she said and half expected
him to pull away. ''Your sister's fighting for her life.
I know you want what's best for her, so whenever
you're around her, I want you to be positive, nurtur-
ing and supportive. Okay?''

He nodded curtly but his lips tightened a bit. He
wasn't and never had been used to taking orders or
advice—not from anyone. ''Any questions?''

''Just one,'' he said slowly.

''What?''

''My sister is important to me. Very important.
You know that. So I want to be assured that she's
getting the best medical care that money can buy.
That means the best hospital, the best staff, and especially the best doctor.''

Realizing she was still holding his hand, she let go
and felt a welling sense of disappointment. It wasn't
the first time her ability had been questioned and certainly wouldn't be the last, but for some reason she
had hoped that Thorne McCafferty would trust her
and her dedication. ''What are you trying to say?''
she asked.

''I need to know that the people here, the doctors

assigned to Randi's care are the best in the country—
or the whole damned world for that matter.''

Self-impressed, rich, corporate bastard.

''That's what everyone wants for their loved ones,
Thorne.''

''The difference is,'' he said, ''I can afford it.''

Her heart sank. Why had she thought she recognized a bit of tenderness in his eyes? Foolish, foolish,
idealistic woman. ''I'm a damned good doctor,
Thorne. So are the others here. This hospital has won
awards. It's small but attracts the best, I can personally assure you of that. Doctors who have once practiced in major cities from Atlanta to Seattle, New
York to L.A., have ended up here because they were
tired of the rat race....'' She let her words sink in and
wished she'd just bitten her tongue. Thorne could
think whatever he damn well pleased.

''Let's go inside. Now, remember, keep it positive
and when I say time's up, don't argue. Just leave. You
can see her again tomorrow.'' She waited, but he
didn't offer any response or protest, just clenched his
jaw so hard a muscle jumped. ''Got it?'' she asked.

''Got it.''

''Then we'll get along just fine,'' she said, but she
didn't believe it for a minute. Some things didn't
change and she and Thorne McCafferty were like oil
and water—they would never mix; never agree.

She pressed a button and placed her face in the
window so that a nurse inside could see her, then
waited to be admitted. As the electronic doors
hummed open, she felt Thorne's gaze center on the
back of her neck beneath the upsweep of her hair.
Without making a sound, he followed her inside. She

wondered how long he'd obey the hospital's and the doctor's terms.

The answer, she knew, was blindingly simple.

Not long enough.

Thorne McCafferty hadn't changed. He was the type of man who played by his own rules.

Chapter Two

Oh, God, this couldn't *be Randi.* Thorne gazed down at the small, inert form lying on the bed and he felt sick inside—weak. Tubes and wires ran from the her body to monitors and equipment with gauges and digital readouts that he didn't understand. Her head was wrapped in gauze, her body draped in sterile-looking sheets, one leg elevated and surrounded by a partial cast. The portions of her face that he could see were bruised and swollen.

His throat was thick with emotion as he stood in the tiny sheet-draped cubicle that opened at the foot of the bed to the nurse's station. His fists clenched impotently, and a quiet, damning rage burned through his soul. How could this have happened? What was she doing up at Glacier Park? Why had her vehicle slid off the road?

The heart monitor beeped softly and steadily yet he wasn't reassured as he stared down at this stranger who was his half sister. A dozen memories darted wildly through his mind and though at one time, when she was first born, he'd been envious and resentful of his father's namesake, he'd never been able to really dislike her.

Randi had been so outgoing and alive, her eyes sparkling with mischief, her laughter contagious, a girl who wore her heart on her sleeve. Guileless and believing that she had every right to be the apple of her father's eye, Randi Penelope McCafferty had bull-dozed her way through life and into almost anyone's heart she came across—including those of her reluctant, hellions of half brothers who had sworn while their new stepmother was pregnant that they would despise the baby who, as far as their tunnel-visioned young eyes could see, was the reason their own parents had divorced so bitterly.

Now, twenty-six years later, Thorne cringed at his ill-focused hostility. He'd been thirteen when his half sister had summoned the gall to arrive, red-faced and screaming into this world. Thorne had been thoroughly disgusted at the thought of his father and the younger woman he'd married actually "doing it" and creating this love child. Worse yet was the scandal surrounding her birth date, barely six months after J. Randall's second nuptials. It had been too humiliating to think about and he'd taken a lot of needling from his classmates who, having always been envious of the McCafferty name, wealth and reputation, had found some dark humor in the situation.

Hell, it had been a long time ago and now, standing

LISA JACKSON 33

in the sterile hospital unit with patients barely clinging to life, his own sister hooked up to machines that helped her survive, Thorne felt a fool. All the mortification and shame Thorne had endured at Randi's conception and birth had disappeared from the first time he'd caught his first real glimpse of her little, innocent face.

Staring into that fancy lace-covered bassinet in the master bedroom at the ranch, Thorne had been ready to hate the baby on sight. After all, for five or six months she'd been the source of all his anger and humiliation. But Thorne had been instantly taken with the little infant with her dark hair, bright eyes and flailing fists. She'd looked as mad to be there as he'd felt that she'd disrupted his life. She'd wailed and cried and put up a fuss that couldn't be believed. The sound that had been emitted from her tiny voice box—like a wounded cougar—had bored right to the heart of him.

He'd hidden his feelings, kept his fascination with the baby to himself and made sure no one, least of all his brothers and father knew how he really felt about the infant, that he'd been beguiled by her from the very beginning of her life.

Now, as he watched her labored breathing and noticed the blood-encrusted bandages that were placed over her swollen face, he felt like a heel. He'd let her slip away from him, hadn't kept in touch because it hadn't been convenient for either of them and now she lay helpless, the victim of an accident that hadn't yet been explained to him.

"You can talk to her," a soft, feminine voice said to him and he looked up to see Nicole looking at him with round, compassionate eyes. The color of aged whiskey and surrounded by thick lashes, they seemed to stare right to his very soul. As they had when he was twenty-two and she'd been barely seventeen. God, that seemed a lifetime ago. "No one knows if she can hear you or not, but it certainly wouldn't hurt." Her lips curved into a tender, encouraging smile and though he felt like a fool, he nodded, surprised not only that she'd matured into a full-fledged woman—but that she was a doctor, no less, and one who could bark out orders or offer compassionate whispers with an equal amount of command. This was Nikki Sanders, the girl who had nearly roped his heart? The one girl who had nearly convinced him to stay in Grand Hope and scrape out a living on the ranch? Leaving her had been tough, but he'd done it. He'd had to.

As if sensing he might need some privacy, she turned back to the chart on which she was taking notes.

Thorne dragged his gaze from the curve of Nikki's neck, though he couldn't help but notice that one strand of gold-streaked hair fell from the knot she'd pinned at her crown. Maybe she wasn't so buttoned-down after all.

Grabbing the cool metal railing at the side of Randi's hospital bed, he concentrated on his sister again. He cleared his throat. "Randi?" he whispered, feeling like an utter fool. "Hey, kid, can you hear me? It's me. Thorne." He swallowed hard as she lay motionless. Old memories flashed through his mind in a kaleidoscope of pictures. It had been Thorne who had found her crying after she'd fallen off her bike when she'd been learning to ride at five. He'd returned home from college for a quick visit, had discovered her at the edge of the lane, her knees scraped, her cheeks dusty and tracked with tears, her pride bitterly wounded as she couldn't get the hang of the two-wheeler. After carrying her to the house, Thorne had plucked the gravel from her knees, then fixed the bent wheel of her bike and helped her keep the damned two-wheeler from toppling every time she tried to learn.

When Randi had been around nine or ten, Thorne had spent an afternoon teaching her how to throw a baseball like a boy—a curveball and a slider. She'd spent hours working at it, throwing that damned old ball at the side of the barn until the paint had peeled off.

Years later, Thorne had returned home one weekend to find his tomboy of a half sister dressed in a long pink dress as she'd waited for her date to the senior prom. Her hair, a rich mahogany color, had been twisted onto the top of her head. She'd stood tall on high heels with a poise and beauty that had shocked him. Around her neck she'd worn a gold chain with the same locket J. Randall had given Randi's mother on their wedding day. Randi had been downright breathtaking. Exuberant. Full of life.

And now she lay unmoving, unconscious, her body battered as she struggled to breathe.

Nicole returned to the side of the bed. Gently she shone a penlight into Randi's eyes, then touched Randi's bare wrist with probing, professional fingers. Little worry lines appeared between her sharply arched brows. Her upper teeth sank into her lower lip as if she were deep in thought. It was an unconsciously sexy movement and he looked away quickly, disgusted at the turn of his thoughts.

From the corner of his eye he noticed her making notations on Randi's chart as she moved to the central area where a nurse's station had full view of all of the patients' beds. Like spokes of a wheel the separated "rooms" radiated from the central desk area. Pale-green privacy drapes separated each bed from the others and nurses in soft-soled shoes moved quietly from one area to the next.

"Why don't you try to speak with her again?" Nicole suggested quietly, not even glancing his way.

He felt so awkward. So out of place. So big. So damned healthy.

"Go on," she encouraged, then turned her back on him completely.

His fingers tightened over the rail. What could he say? What did it matter? Thorne leaned forward, closer to the bed where his sister lay so still. "Randi," he whispered in a voice that nearly cracked with emotions he tried desperately to repress. He touched one of her fingers and she didn't respond, didn't move. "Can ya hear me? Well, you'd better." Hell, he was bad at this sort of thing. He shifted so that his fingers laced with hers. "How ya doin'?"

Of course she didn't answer and as the heart monitor beeped a steady, reassuring beat, he wished to heaven that he'd been a better older brother to her, that he'd been more involved with her life. He noticed the soft rounding of her abdomen beneath the sheet stretched over her belly. She'd been pregnant. Now had a child. A mother at twenty-six. Yet no one in the family knew of any man with whom she'd been involved. "Can...can you hear me? Huh, kiddo?"

Oh, this was inane. She wasn't going to respond. Couldn't. He doubted she heard a word he said, or sensed that he was near. He felt like a fool and yet he was stuck like proverbial glue, adhering to her, their fingers linked, as if someway he could force some of his sheer brute strength into her tiny body, could by his indomitable will make her strong, healthy and safe.

He caught a glance from Nicole, an unspoken word that told him his time was up.

Clearing his throat again, he pulled his hand from hers, then gently tapped the end of her index finger with his. "You hang in there, okay? Matt, Slade and I, we're all pulling for you, kid, so you just give it your best. And you've got a baby, now—a little boy who needs you. Like we all do, kid." *Oh, hell, this was impossible. Ludicrous.* And yet he said, "I, uh, I—we're all pullin' for you and I'll be back soon. Promise." The last word nearly cracked.

Randi didn't move and the back of Thorne's eyes burned in a way they hadn't since the day he learned his father had died. Shoving his hands into the pockets of his coat, he crossed the room and walked through the doors that opened as he approached. He sensed, rather than saw Nicole as she joined him.

"Give it to me straight," he said as they strode along a corridor with bright lights and windows overlooking a parking lot. Outside it was dark as night, black clouds showering rain that puddled on the asphalt and dripped from the few scraggly trees that were planted near the building. "What are her chances?"

Nicole's steps, shorter by half than his own, were quick. She managed to keep up with him though her brow was knitted, her eyes narrowed in thought. "She's young and strong. She has as good a chance as anyone."

An aide pushing a man in a wheelchair passed them going the opposite direction and somewhere a phone rang. Piped-in music competed with the hum of soft conversation and the muted rattle of equipment being wheeled down other corridors. As they reached the elevator, Thorne touched Nicole lightly on the elbow.

"I want to know if my sister is going to make it."

Color flushed her cheeks. "I don't have a crystal ball, you know, Thorne. I realize that you and your brothers want precise, finite answers. I just don't have them. It's too early."

"But she will live?" he asked, desperate to be reassured. He, who was always in control, was hanging on the words of a small woman whom he'd once come close to loving.

"As I said before, barring any unforeseen—"

"I heard you the first time. Just tell me the truth. Point-blank. Is my sister going to make it?"

She looked about to launch into him, then took a deep breath. "I believe so. We're all doing everything possible for her." As if reading the concern in his eyes, she sighed and rubbed the kinks from the back of her neck. Her face softened a bit and he couldn't help but notice the lines of strain surrounding her eyes, the intelligence in those gorgeous amber-colored irises and he felt the same male interest he had years ago, when she was a senior in high school. "Look, I'm sorry. I don't mean to be evasive. Really." She tucked an errant lock of hair behind her ear. "I wish I could tell you that Randi will be fine, that within a couple of weeks she'll be up walking around, laughing, going back to work, taking care of that baby of hers and that everything will be all right. But I can't do that. She's suffered a lot of trauma. Internal organs are damaged, bones broken. Her concussion is more than just a little bump on her head. I won't kid you. There's a chance that if she does survive, there may be brain damage. We just don't know yet."

His heart nearly stopped. He'd feared for his sister's life, but never once considered that she might survive only to live her life with less mental capabilities than she had before. She'd always been so smart—"Sharp as a tack," their father had bragged often enough.

"Shouldn't she see a specialist?" Thorne asked.

"She's seeing several. Doctor Nimmo is one of the best neurosurgeons in the Northwest. He's already examined her. He usually works out of Bitterroot Memorial and just after Randi's surgery he was called away on another emergency, but he'll phone you. Believe me. Your sister's getting the best medical care we can provide, and it's as good as you're going to get anywhere. I think we've already had this conversation, so you're just going to have to trust me. Now, is there anything else?"

"Just that I want to be kept apprised of her situation. If there is any change, any change at all in her condition or that of the child, I expect to be contacted immediately." He withdrew his wallet and slid a crisp business card from the smooth leather. "This is my business phone number and this—" he found a pen in the breast pocket of his suit jacket and scribbled another number on the back of his card "—is the number of the ranch. I'll be staying there." He handed her the card and watched as one of her finely arched brows elevated a bit.

"You expect *me* to contact you. Me, personally."

"I—I'd appreciate it," he said and touched her shoulder. She glanced down at his hand and little lines converged between her eyebrows. "As a personal favor."

Her lips pulled into a tight knot. Color stained her cheeks. "Because we were so close to each other?" she asked, gold eyes snapping as she pulled her shoulder away.

He dropped his hand. "Because you care. I don't know the rest of the staff and I'm sure that they're fine. All good doctors. But I *know* I can trust you."

"You don't know me at all."

"I did once."

She swallowed hard. "Let's keep that out of this," she said. "But, fine…I'll keep you informed."

"Thanks." He offered her a smile and she rolled her eyes.

"Just don't try to smooth-talk or con me, Thorne, okay? I'll tell it to you straight, but don't, not for a minute, try to play on my sympathies and, just to make sure you're getting this, I'm not doing it for old times' sake or anything the least bit maudlin or nostalgic, okay? If there's a change, you'll be notified immediately."

"And I'll be in contact with you."

"I'm not her doctor, Thorne."

"But you'll be here."

"Most of the time. Now, if you'll excuse me, I've really got to run." She started to turn away, but he caught the crook of her elbow, his fingers gripping the starched white coat.

"Thanks, Nikki," he said and to his amazement she blushed, a deep shade of pink stealing up her cheeks.

"No problem. It comes with the job," she said, then glanced down at his fingers and pulled away. With clipped steps she disappeared through a door marked Staff Only. Thorne watched the door swing shut behind her and fought the urge to ignore the warning and follow her. Why he couldn't imagine. There was nothing more to say—the conversation was finished, but as he tucked his wallet back into his pocket, he experienced a foolish need to catch up with her—to catch up with his past. He had dozens of questions for her and he'd probably never ask one. "Fool," he muttered to himself and felt a headache begin to pound at the base of his skull. Nicole Stevenson was a doctor here at the hospital, nothing more. And she had his number. Big time. She'd made that clear enough.

Yes, she was a woman; a beautiful woman, a smart woman, a seemingly driven woman, a woman with whom he'd made love once upon a time, but their affair was long over.

And she could be married, you idiot. Her name is Stevenson now, remember?

But he'd checked her ring finger. It had been bare.

Why he'd bothered, he didn't understand; didn't want
to assess. But he was satisfied that she was no longer
another man's wife. Nonetheless she was off-limits.
Period. A complicated, beguiling woman.

He stepped onto the elevator, pounded the button
for the floor of the maternity level and tried to shove
all thoughts of Nikki Sanders—Dr. Nicole Stevenson—from his mind.

But it didn't work; just as it hadn't worked years
before when he'd left her. Without so much as an
explanation. How could he have explained that he'd
left her because staying in Grand Hope, being close
to her, touching her and loving her made his departure
all that much harder? He'd left because he'd had a
deep sense of insight that if he'd stayed much longer,
he would never have been able to tear himself away
from her, that he never would have gone out into the
world and proved to himself and his father that he
could make his own mark.

"Hell," he cursed. He'd been a fool and let the
only woman who had come close to touching a part
of him he didn't want to know existed—that nebulous
essence that was his soul—get away from him. He'd
figured that out a couple of years later, but Thorne
had never been one to look back and second-guess
himself. He'd told himself there would be another
woman someday—when he was ready.

Of course he'd never found her.

And he hadn't even worried about it until he'd seen
Nikki Sanders again, remembered how it felt to kiss
her, and the phrase *what if* had entered his mind. If
he'd stuck by her, married her, had children by her,

his father wouldn't have gone to his grave without grandchildren. "Stop it," he growled to himself.

Nicole let out her breath as she walked through the maze that was St. James. She was still unsettled and shaken. Used to dealing with anxious, sometimes even grieving relatives, she hadn't expected that she would have such an intense and disturbing reaction to Thorne McCafferty.

"He's just a man," she grumbled, taking the stairs. "That's all."

But she met men every day of the week. All kinds from all walks of life and none of them caused anywhere near this kind of response.

Was it because he had been her first lover? Because he nearly broke her heart? Because he left her, not because of another woman, not because he had any good reason, just because she didn't mean enough to him?

"Fool," she muttered under her breath as she pushed open the door to the floor where her office was housed.

"Excuse me?" a janitor who was walking down the hall asked.

"Nothing. Talking to myself." She offered the man an embarrassed smile and continued to her office where she plopped into her desk chair and stared at the monitor of her computer. The notes that had filled her head only an hour earlier seemed scattered to the wind and she couldn't budge thoughts of Thorne from her brain. In her silly, very feminine mind's eye she saw him with the clarity of young, loving eyes. Oh, she'd adored him. He was older. Sophisticated. Rich.

One of the McCafferty scoundrels—bad boys every one, who had been known to womanize, smoke, drink and generally raise hell in their youths.

Handsome, arrogant and cocky, Thorne had found easy access to her naive heart. The only daughter of a poor, hardworking woman who pushed for and expected perfection, Nicole had, at seventeen, been ripe for rebellion. And then she'd stumbled onto Thorne.

She'd fallen stupidly head over heels in love, nearly throwing all of her own hopes and dreams away on the rakish college boy.

Blowing her bangs out of her eyes she shook her head to dislodge those old, painful and humiliating memories. She'd been so young. So mindlessly sophomoric, caught up in romantic fantasies with the least likely candidate for a long-term relationship in the state.

"Don't even think about it," she reminded herself, moving the mouse of her computer and studying the screen while memories of making love to him under the star-studded Montana sky swept through her mind. His body had been young, hard, muscular and sheened in sweat. His eyes had been silver with the moon glow, his hair unkempt.

And now he was some kind of corporate hotshot.

Like Paul. She glanced down at her hands and was relieved to see that the groove her wedding ring had once carved in her finger had disappeared in the past two years. Paul Stevenson had been climbing the corporate ladder so fast, he'd lost track of his wife and young daughters.

She suspected Thorne wasn't much different.

When she'd moved back to Grand Hope a year ago, she'd known his family was still scattered around the state, but she'd thought Thorne was long gone and hadn't expected to come face-to-face with him. According to the rumors circulating through Grand Hope like endless eddies and whirlpools, Thorne had finished law school, linked up with a firm in Missoula, then moved to California and finally wound up in Denver where he was the executive for a multinational corporation. He'd never married, had no children that anyone knew of, and had been linked to several beautiful, wealthy, career-minded women over the years, none of whom had lasted on his arm too long before they'd been replaced with a newer model.

Yep. Thorne was a lot like Paul.

Except that you're still attracted to him, aren't you? One look, and your gullible heart started pounding all over again.

"Stop it!" she growled and forced herself to concentrate. This wasn't like her. She'd been known to be single-minded when it came to her work or her children and she found the distraction of Thorne McCafferty more than a little disconcerting. She couldn't, *wouldn't* fall victim to his insidious charms again. With renewed conviction, she ignored any lingering thoughts of Thorne and undid the clasp holding her hair in place. No doubt she'd have to deal with him later and at the thought her heart alternately leaped and sank. "Great," she told herself as she finger-combed her hair, "Just…great."

Right now facing Thorne again seemed an insurmountable challenge.

Twenty minutes later Thorne was still smarting from the tongue-lashing he'd received from a very

sturdily built and strong-willed nurse who allowed
him one glimpse of Randi's infant, then ushered him
out of the pediatric intensive care unit. Thorne had
peered through thick glass to an airy room where two
newborns were sleeping in plastic bassinets. Randi's
boy had lain under lamps, a shock of red-blond hair
sticking upward, his tiny lips moving slightly as he
breathed. To his utter surprise, Thorne had felt an
unexpected pull on his heartstrings and he'd promptly
advised himself that idiocy ran in the McCafferty
family. Nonetheless Thorne had stared at the baby, so
tiny, so mystifying, so innocent and unaware of all
the turmoil he had caused.

As he'd left the pediatric unit Thorne wondered
about the man who had fathered the child. Who was
he? Shouldn't he be contacted? Was Randi in love
with him? Or…had she hidden her pregnancy and the
fact that she was involved with someone from her
brothers for a reason?

Thorne didn't care. He'd find out about the kid's
father if it killed him. And he couldn't sit idle just
waiting for Randi to recover. No, there was too much
to do. Ramming his hands into his coat pockets, he
took a flight of stairs to the first floor.

"Think," he ordered himself and a plan started
forming in his mind. First he had to make sure that
both Randi and her child were on the road to recovery, then he'd hire a private investigator to look into
his sister's life. Wincing at the thought of prying into
Randi's private business, he rationalized that he had
no choice. In her current state, Randi couldn't help
herself. Nor could she care for her child.

Thorne would have to locate the baby's father, in-

LISA JACKSON   47

terview the son of a bitch, then set up a trust fund for
the kid.

Already planning how to attack the "Randi situation" as he'd begun to think of it, he shouldered open
a door to the parking lot. Outside, the wind raged.
Ice-cold raindrops beat down from a leaden sky. He
hiked his collar more closely around his neck and
ducked his head. Skirting puddles, he strode toward
his vehicle—a Ford pickup that was usually garaged
at the ranch's airstrip.

Then he saw her.

Running to her car, her briefcase held over her
head, Dr. Nicole Stevenson—Nikki Sanders once
upon a time—dashed toward a white four-wheel-drive
that was parked in a nearby lot.

Rain ran down his neck and dripped off his nose
as he watched her. Her hair was no longer pinned to
the back of her head, but caught in the wind. Her stark
white lab coat had been replaced by a long leather
jacket cinched firmly around her waist.

Without thinking, Thorne swept across the puddle-
strewn lot. "Nikki!"

She looked up and he was stunned. "Oh. Thorne."
With raindrops caught in the sweep of her eyelashes
and her blond-streaked hair tossed around her face in
soft layers, she was more gorgeous than he remembered. Raindrops slipped down sculpted cheekbones
to a small mouth that was set in a startled pout.

For a split second he thought of kissing her, but
quickly shoved that ridiculous thought from his mind.

She jabbed her key into the SUV's lock. "What're
you doing lurking around out here?"

"Maybe I was waiting for you," he said automatically—actually *flirting* with her. For the love of God, what had gotten into him?

He saw her eyes round a bit, then one corner of her mouth lifted in sarcasm. "Try again."

"Okay, how about this? I just got finished dealing with Nurse Ratched up in Pediatrics and was tossed out on my ear."

"Someone intimidated you?" One eyebrow lifted in disbelief. "I don't think so." If she'd been teasing him before, she'd obviously thought better of it and her smile fell away. She yanked open the door and the interior light blinked on. "Now...was there something you wanted?"

You, he thought, then chided himself. What the devil was he thinking? What they'd shared was long over. "I didn't get your home number."

"I didn't give it to you."

"Because of your husband?"

"What? No." She shook her head. "There is no husband, not anymore." She was standing between the car and open door, waiting, her hair turning dark with the rain. His heart raced. She was single. "You can reach me here," she said. "If it's an emergency, the hospital will page me."

"I'd feel better if I could—"

"Look, Thorne," she said pointedly. "I understand that you're a man used to getting your way, of being in charge, of making things happen, but this time you can't, okay? At least not with me, not any more, nor with St. James Hospital. So, if there's nothing else, you'll have to excuse me." Her eyes weren't the least bit warm and yet her lips, slick with rainwater just begged to be kissed.

And, damn it, he reacted. Knowing that she'd probably slap him silly, he grabbed her, hauled her body close to his and bent his head so that his lips were suspended just above hers. "Okay, Nikki," he said as he felt her tense. "I excuse you." Then he kissed her, pressed his mouth over hers and felt a second's surrender when her lips parted and her breath mingled with his as rain drenched them both. The scent of her perfume teased his nostrils and memories of making love to her over and over again burned through his brain. Dear God, how she'd responded to him then, just as she was now. He was lost in the feel of her and old emotions escaped from the place where he'd so steadfastly locked them long ago. With a groan, he kissed her harder, deeper, his arms tightening around her.

Her entire body stiffened. She jerked her head away as if she'd been burned. "Don't," she warned, her voice husky, her lips trembling a bit. She swallowed hard, then leaned back to glare up at him. "Don't ever do this again. This—" she raised a hand only to let it fall "—this was uncalled for and…and entirely…*entirely* inappropriate."

"Entirely," he agreed, not releasing her.

"I mean it, Thorne."

"Why? Because I scare you?"

"Because whatever you and I shared together is over."

He lifted a doubting eyebrow as rain drizzled down his face. "Then why—?"

"Over!" Her eyes narrowed and she pulled out of

his embrace. Though he wanted nothing more than to drag her close again, he let her go and tamped down the fire that had stormed through his blood, the pulse of lust that had thudded in his brain and caused a heat to burn in his loins. "I don't know what happened to you in the past seventeen years, but believe me, you should take some lessons in subtlety."

"Should I? Maybe you could give them to me."

"Me?" She let out a whisper of a laugh. "Right. Just don't hold your breath."

She slid into the interior of the car and reached for the door handle. Before she could yank the door closed, he said, "Okay, maybe I was outta line."

"Oh? You think?"

"I know."

"Good, then it won't happen again." She crammed her key into the ignition, muttered something about self-important bullheaded men, twisted her wrist and sent him a look that was meant to cut to the quick. The SUV's engine sputtered, then died. "Don't do this to me," she said and he wondered if she was talking to him or her rig. "Don't do this to me now." She turned the key again and the engine ground but didn't catch. "Damn."

"If you need a ride—"

"It'll start. It's just temperamental."

"Like its owner."

"If you say so." She took a deep breath, snapped her seat belt into place and grabbed the handle of her door. "Good night, Thorne." She yanked the door closed, turned the key again and finally the rig roared to life. Pressing on the gas pedal, she revved the engine and rolled down the window. "I'll let you know

if there are any changes in your sister's condition.''
With that she tore out of the parking lot and Thorne,
watching the taillights disappear, mentally kicked
himself.

He'd been a fool to grab her.

And yet he knew he'd do it again.

If given half a chance.

Yep, he'd do it in a heartbeat.

Chapter Three

"God help me," Nicole whispered, trying to understand why in the world Thorne would embrace her so intimately and more to the point, why didn't she stop him. *Because you wanted him to, you idiot.*

As she wheeled out of the parking lot, she glanced in the rearview mirror, and saw him standing beneath a security light. Tall, broad-shouldered, bareheaded, rain dripping from the tip of his nose and the hem of his coat, he watched her leave. "Cocky son of a gun," she muttered, flipping on her blinker and joining the thin stream of traffic. She hoped Thorne Almighty McCafferty got soaked to the skin. She switched her windshield wipers to a faster pace to keep up with the rain. Who was he to barge in on her, to question her and the hospital's integrity and then...and then have the audacity, the sheer arrogance, to grab her as if she were some weak-willed, starry-eyed, spineless...ninny!

Oh, like the girl you once were, the one he remembered?

She blushed and her fingers curled around the steering wheel in a death grip. She'd worked hard for years to overcome her shyness, to become the confident, scholarly, take-charge emergency room physician she was today and Thorne McCafferty seemed hell-bent to change all that. Well, she wouldn't let him. No way. No how. She wasn't the little girl he'd left a lifetime ago—her broken heart had mended.

As she braked for a red light, she flipped on the radio, fumbled with the stations until she heard a melody that was familiar—Whitney Houston singing something she should know—and tried to calm down. Why she let Thorne get to her, she didn't understand.

She cranked the wheel and turned into a side street where the neon lights and Western facade of Montana Joe's Pizza Parlor came into view.

She pulled into the lot, raced inside and waited in line between five or six other patrons whose raincoats, parkas and ski jackets dripped water onto the tile floor in front of the take-out counter. A gas flame hissed in the fireplace in one corner of the room that was divided by fences into different seating areas. Pickaxes and shovels and other mining memorabilia were tacked to bare cedar walls and in one corner, Montana Joe, a stuffed bison, stared with glassy eyes at the patrons who were listening to Garth Brooks's latest hit while drinking beer and eating hot, stringy pizza made with Joe's "secret" tomato sauce.

As Nicole stood in line and dug into her wallet to

check how much cash she was carrying, she couldn't help but overhear some of the conversation of the other patrons. Two men in front of her were discussing the previous Friday's high school football game. From the sound of it the Grand Hope Wolverines were edged out by an arch rival in a nearby town though there was some dispute over a few of the calls. Typical.

Other conversations buzzed around her and she heard the name McCafferty more often than she wanted to. ''Terrible accident…half sister, you know…pregnant, but no mention of a father and no husband…always was bad blood in that family…what goes around comes around, I tell you…''

Nicole grabbed a menu from the counter and turned her attention from the gossip that swirled around her. Though Grand Hope had grown by leaps and bounds in the past few years and had become a major metropolis by Montana standards, it was still, at its heart, a small town, where many of the citizens knew each other. She placed her order, lingered near the jukebox and listened to a three or four songs ranging from Patsy Cline to Wynona Judd, then, once her name was called, picked up her pizza and refused to think about any member of the McCafferty family—especially Thorne. He was off-limits. Period. The reason she'd responded to his kiss was simple. It had been over two years since she'd kissed any man and at least five since she'd felt even the tiniest spark of passion. She didn't even want to think how long it had been since she'd been consumed with desire—that particular thought led her back to a path that she didn't want to follow, a path heading straight back to her youth and

Thorne. She was just susceptible right now, that was all. Nothing more. It had nothing to do with chemistry. Nothing.

Once in her SUV again, she twisted on the key and the engine refused to fire. "Come on, come on," she muttered. She tried again, pumping the gas frantically and mentally chiding herself for not taking the rig into the shop for its regular maintenance. "You can do it," she encouraged and finally, on the fourth attempt, the engine caught. "Tomorrow," she promised, patting the dash as if comforting the vehicle, as if that would help. "I'll take you in. Promise."

On the road again, Nicole drove through the side streets to her little cottage on the outskirts of town. Her stomach rumbled as the tangy scents of melting cheese and spicy sauce filled the rig's interior and her mind, damn it, ran back to Thorne and the feel of his lips on hers. He was everything she despised in a man: arrogant, competitive, in control and determined—a real corporate Type A and the kind of man she had learned to avoid like the plague. But beneath his layer of pride and his take-charge mentality, she'd caught glimpses of a more complex man, a gentler soul who stumbled through the awkwardness of talking to his comatose sister. He'd tried to communicate with Randi, the back of his neck flushing in embarrassment, his steely gray eyes conveying a sense of raw pain at his sister's condition—as if he somehow blamed himself for her accident.

"Don't read more into it than there is," she warned herself as she cranked the wheel and braked in her driveway. She pulled to a stop in front of her garage and made a mental note that between helping at preschool, the twins' dance lessons, the housework and the grocery shopping, she should call a roofer for a bid on the sagging roof.

Juggling her briefcase and boxed pizza, she made a mad dash to the back porch and was able to unlock the door, then shove it open with her hip.

Patches, her black-and-white cat, streaked through the opening and Nicole nearly tripped on the speeding feline. Tiny footsteps thundered through the house. "Mommy! Mommy! Mommy!" the twins cried, flying pell-mell into the kitchen and sliding on the yellowed linoleum as Patches slunk down the bedroom hallway. Molly and Mindy were dressed in identical pink-and-white-checked sleepers that zipped up the front and covered their feet in attached slippers. Their hair was wet and curled in dark-brown ringlets around cherubic faces and bright brown eyes.

Nicole slid the pizza onto a counter, knelt and opened her arms wide. The four-year-old imps nearly bowled her over. "Miss me?" she asked.

"Yeth," Mindy said shyly, nodding her head and smiling.

"You got pizza?" Molly demanded. "I'm hungry."

"I sure do. Lots of it." She dropped kisses on each wet head, then standing once again, she stripped out of her coat and hung it in a tiny closet near the eating alcove.

Jenny Riley appeared in the archway separating the kitchen from the dining room. Tall and willowy, with long straight black hair and a nose ring, the twenty-year-old had been the twins' nanny since Nicole had moved to Grand Hope.

"How were they today?" Nicole asked.

"Miserable as usual," Jenny said, her green eyes twinkling, sarcasm lacing her words.

"Were not!" Molly said, planting her little fists on her hips. "We was good."

"Were," Nicole corrected. "You were good."

"Yeth," Mindy said, nodding agreement with her precocious sister. "Real good."

Jenny laughed and bent down to retie the laces of her elevated tennis shoes, "Oh, okay, I lied," she admitted. "You were good. Both of you. Very good."

"It's not nice to lie!" Molly said with a toss of her wet curls.

"I know, I know, it won't happen again," Jenny promised, straightening and slinging the strap of her fringed leather purse over her shoulder.

"Want a piece of pizza?" Nicole offered. Using her fingers and a spatula she'd grabbed from a hook over the stove, she slid piping hot slices onto paper plates. The girls scrambled onto the booster seats. Nicole licked a piece of melted cheese from her fingers and looked questioningly at Jenny.

"No thanks, Mom's got dinner waiting and—" Jenny winked broadly "—I've got a hot date after."

"Oooh," Nicole said, licking gooey cheese from her fingers. "Anyone I know?"

"Nope. Not unless you're into twenty-two-year-old cowboys."

"Only in the ER. I have been known to treat them upon occasion."

"Not this one," Jenny said with a wide grin and slight blush.

"Tell me more."

"His name is Adam. He's a hired hand at the McCafferty spread. And...I'll fill you in more later."

Nicole's good mood vanished at the mention of the McCaffertys. Today, it seemed, she couldn't avoid them for a minute.

"Gotta run," Jenny said as Molly reached across the table to peel off pieces of pepperoni from her sister's slice of pizza.

Mindy sent up a wail guaranteed to wake the dead in every cemetery in the county. "No!" she cried. "Mommeee!"

Grinning, Molly dangled all the pilfered slices of pepperoni over her open mouth before dropping them onto her tongue. Gleefully she chewed them in front of her sister.

"I'm outta here," Jenny said and slipped through the door as Nicole tried to right the wrong and Patches, appearing from the hallway, had the nerve to hop onto the counter near the microwave.

"You, down!" Nicole said, clapping her hands loudly. The cat leaped to the floor and darted in a black-and-white streak into the living room. "Everyone seems to have an attitude today." She turned her attention back to the twins and pointed at Molly. "Don't touch your sister's food."

"She's not eating it," Molly argued while chewing.

"Am, too!" Big tears rolled down Mindy's face.

"But it's hers and—"

"And we're s'posed to share. You said so."

"Not your food...well, not now. You know better. Now, come on, there's no real harm done here." Nicole picked off pepperoni slices from another piece of pizza and placed them on the half-eaten wedge that sat on Mindy's plate. "Good as new."

But the damage was done. Mindy wouldn't stop sobbing and pointing a condemning finger at her twin. "You, bad!"

Molly shook her head. "Am not."

Nicole shot her outspoken daughter a look meant to silence her, then picked Mindy up and, consoling her while walking toward the hallway, whispered into her ear, "Come on, big girl, let's brush your teeth and get you into bed."

"Don't wanna—" Mindy complained and Molly cackled loudly before realizing she was alone. Quickly she slid out of her chair and little feet pounding, ran after Nicole and Mindy. In the bathroom, the dispute was forgotten, tears were wiped away and two sets of teeth were brushed. As the pizza cooled, mozzarella cheese congealing, Nicole and the girls spent the next twenty minutes cuddled beneath a quilt in her grandmother's old rocker. She read them two stories they'd heard a dozen times before. Mindy's eyes immediately shut while Molly, ever the fighter, struggled to stay awake only to drop off a few minutes later.

For the first time that day, Nicole felt at peace. She eyed the fire that Jenny had built earlier. Dying embers and glowing coals in deep ashes were all that remained to light the little living room in shades of gold and red. Humming, she rocked until she too, nearly dozed off.

Struggling out of the chair she managed to carry her daughters into their bedroom and tuck them into matching twin beds. Mindy yawned and rolled over, her thumb moving instinctively to her mouth and Molly blinked twice, said, "I love you, Mommy," then fell asleep again.

"Me, too, baby. Me, too." She kissed each daughter and smelled the scents of shampoo and baby powder, then walked softly to the door.

Molly sighed loudly. Mindy smacked her little lips.

Folding her arms over her chest Nicole leaned against the doorjamb.

Her ex-husband's words, "You'll never make it on your own," echoed through her mind and she felt her spine stiffen. *Right, Paul,* she thought now, *but I'm not on my own. I've got the kids. And I'm going to make it. On my own.*

Every minute of that painful, doomed marriage was worth it because she had the girls. They were a family—maybe not an old-fashioned, traditional, 1950s sitcom family, but a family nonetheless.

She thought fleetingly of Randi's baby, tucked away in the maternity ward, his father not yet found, his mother in a coma and she wondered what would become of the little boy.

But the baby has Thorne and Matt and Slade. Between the three of them, certainly the boy would be taken care of. Every one of the McCafferty brothers seemed interested in the child, but each one of them was a bachelor—how confirmed, she didn't know.

"Not that it matters," she reminded herself and glanced outside where rain was dripping from the gutters and splashing against the window. She thought of Thorne again, of the way his lips felt against hers, and she realized that she had to avoid being alone with him. She had to keep their relationship professional because she knew from experience that Thorne was trouble.

Big trouble.

He was making a mistake of incredible proportions and he knew it, but he couldn't stop himself. Driving through the city streets and silently marveling at how this town had grown, he'd decided to see Nikki again before returning to the ranch. She'd probably throw him out and he really didn't blame her as he'd come on way too strong, but he had to see her again.

After watching her wheel out of the parking lot after their last confrontation, he'd walked back into the hospital, downed a cup of bitter coffee in the cafeteria, then tried to track down any doctor remotely associated with Randi and the baby. He'd struck out with most, left messages on their answering machines and after talking to a nurse in Pediatrics and one in ICU, he'd called the ranch, told Slade that he'd be back soon, then paused at the gift shop in the hospital lobby, bought a single white rose and, ducking his shoulders against the rain, ran outside and climbed into his truck.

"This is nuts," he told himself as he drove across a bridge and into an established part of town, to the address he'd found in the telephone directory when he'd made his calls to the other doctors. Bracing himself for a blistering reception, he parked in front of the small cottage, grabbed the single flower and climbed out of the car.

Jaw set he dashed up the cement walk, and before he could change his mind, pressed on the door buzzer. He'd been in tighter spots than this. He heard noises inside, the sound of feet. The porch light snapped on and he saw her eyebrows and eyes peer through one of the three small windows cut into the door. A moment later they disappeared as, he supposed, she dropped to her flat feet from her tiptoes.

Locks clicked. The door opened. And there she stood, all five feet three of her wrapped in a fluffy white robe. "Is there something I can do for you?" she asked without a smile. Her eyes skated from his face to the flower in his hands.

He nearly laughed. "You know, this seemed like a good idea at the time but now...now I feel like a damned fool."

"Because?" Again the lift of that lofty eyebrow.

"Because I thought I owed you an apology for the way I came on earlier."

"In the parking lot?"

"And the hospital."

"You were upset. Don't worry about it."

"I wasn't just upset. I was, as I said before out of line, and I'd like to make it up to you."

Her chin lifted a fraction. "Make it up to me? With...that?" she asked, one finger pointing to the single white bud.

"To start with." He handed her the flower and thought, beneath her hard posturing, he caught a glimpse of a deeper emotion. She held the flower, lifted it to her nose and sighed.

"Thanks. This is enough...more than you needed to do."

"No, I think I owe you an explanation."

She tensed again. "It was only a kiss. I'll live."

"I mean about the past."

"No!" She was emphatic. "Look, let's just forget it, okay? It's been a long day. For both of us. Thanks for the flower and the apology, it's…it's very nice of you, but I think it would be best—for everyone, including your sister and her new baby—if we both just pretended that nothing ever happened between us."

"Can you?"

"Y-yes. Of course."

He couldn't stop one side of his mouth from twitching upward. "Liar," he said and Nicole nearly took a step backward. Who was he to stop by her house and…and *what? Apologize? What's the crime in that? Why don't you ask him in and offer him a cup of coffee or a drink?*

"No!"

"You're not a liar?"

"Not usually," she said, recovering a bit. She felt the lapel of her bathrobe gap and it took all of her willpower not to clutch it closed like a silly, frightened virgin. "You seem to bring out the worst in me."

"Ditto." He leaned forward and she expected him to kiss her again, but instead of molding his lips to hers, he brushed his mouth across the slope of her cheek in the briefest of touches. "Good night, Doctor," he whispered and then he turned and hurried down the porch steps to dash through the rain.

She stood in the glow of the porch lamp, her fingers curled possessively around the rose's stem and watched him steer his truck around in her driveway before he drove into the night. Forcing herself inside, she closed and bolted the door. She didn't know what was happening, but she was certain it wasn't going to be good.

She couldn't, wouldn't get involved with Thorne again. No way. No how. In fact, she'd toss the damned flower into the garbage right now. Padding to the kitchen she opened the cupboard under the sink, pulled out the trash can and hesitated. How childish. Thorne was trying to make amends. Nothing more. She touched the side of her cheek, then placed the rosebud in a small vase, certain it would mock her for the next week.

"Don't let him get to you," she warned, but had the fatalistic sensation that it was already too late. He'd gotten to her a long, long time ago.

Thorne parked outside of what had once been the machine shed and eyed the home where he'd been raised, a place he'd once vowed to leave and never return. Though it was dark and the rain was coming down in sheets, he saw the house looming on its small rise, warm patches of light glowing from tall, paned windows. It had been a haven at one time, a prison later.

He grabbed his briefcase and the overnight bag and wondered what had come over him. Why had he stopped at Nikki's? There was more than just a simple apology involved and that thought disturbed him. It was as if seeing her again sparked something deep inside him, something he'd thought had burned out years before, a smoldering ember he hadn't known existed.

Whatever it was, he didn't have time for it and he didn't want to examine it too closely.

Lights blazed from the stables and he recognized Slade's rig parked near the barn. As he ducked through the rain he remembered the first time he'd seen Nicole—years ago at a local Fourth of July celebration in town. He'd been back from college, ready to enter law school in the fall, randy as hell and anxious to get on with his life. She'd only been seventeen, a shy girl with the most incredible eyes he'd ever seen as she'd staked out a spot on a hill overlooking the town and waited for darkness and the fireworks that were planned.

Funny, he hadn't thought of that night in a long, long time. It seemed a million years ago and was tangled up in the other memories that haunted this particular place. As he walked up the front steps he remembered nearly drowning in the swimming hole when he was about eight, hunting pheasants with his brothers and pretending the cold silence between his parents really didn't exist. But the memories that were the clearest, the most poignantly bright, were of Nikki.

"Yeah, well, don't go there," he warned himself as he yanked open the screen door. He walked inside and was greeted by the smells of his youth—soot from the fireplace, fresh lemon wax on the floors, and the lingering aroma of bacon that had been fried earlier in the day and still wisped through the familiar hallways and rooms. He dropped his briefcase and bag near the front door and swiped the rain from his face.

"Thorne?" Matt's voice rang loudly through the century-old house. The sound of boots tripping down the stairs heralded his brother's arrival onto the first floor. "I wondered when you'd show up." Forever in jeans and a flannel shirt with the sleeves rolled up, Matt clapped his brother on the shoulder. "How're you, you old bastard?"

"Same as ever."

"Mean and ornery and on your way to your next million-dollar deal?" Matt asked, as he always did, but this time the question hit a nerve and gave him pause.

"I can only hope," he said, unbuttoning his coat, though it was a lie. He was jaded with his life. Bored. Wanted more. He just wasn't sure what.

"How's Randi?" Matt asked, his face becoming a mask of concern.

"The same as when you saw her. Nothing new to report since I called you from the hospital."

"I guess it's just gonna take time." Matt hitched his chin toward the living room where lamplight filtered into the hallway. "Come on in. I'll buy you a drink. You look like you could use one."

"That bad?"

"We could all use one today."

Thorne nodded. "So where's Slade?"

"Feeding the stock. He'll be in soon. I was just on my way to help him, but since you're here, I figure it won't hurt him to finish the job by himself." Matt flashed his killer smile, the one that had charmed more women than Thorne wanted to count.

Matt had been described as tall, dark and handsome by too many local girls to remember. The middle of the three McCafferty brothers, Matt's eyes were so deep brown they were nearly black, his skin tanned from spending hours outdoors, and the shadow covering his jaw was as dark as their father's had once been.

Sinewy and rawhide tough, Matt McCafferty could bend a horseshoe at a forge as well as he could brand a mustang or rope a maverick calf. Raw. Wild. Stubborn as hell.

Matt belonged here.

Thorne didn't.

Not since his parents had divorced.

"Look at you." Matt gave a sharp whistle. One near-black eyebrow cocked as he fingered the wool of Thorne's coat. "Since when did you become a fashion statement?"

Thorne snorted in derision. "Don't think I am. But I happened to be at work when Slade got hold of me." Thorne hung his coat on an aging brass hook mounted near the door. The long wool overcoat seemed out of place in the array of denim, down and sheepskin jackets. "Didn't have time to change." He pulled at the knot in his tie and let the silk drape over his shoulders. "Tell me what's going on."

"Good question." Together they walked into the living room where the leather couches were worn, an upright piano gathered dust, and two rockers placed at angles near blackened stones of the fireplace remained unmoving. His great-grandfather's rifle was mounted over the mantel, resting on the spikes of antlers from an elk killed long ago. "There's not a lot to tell."

Matt opened the liquor cabinet hidden in cupboards beneath a bookcase filled with leather-backed tomes that hadn't been read in years. "What'll it be?"

"Scotch."

"Straight up?"

"You got it…well, I think."

Matt scrounged around in the cabinet and with a snort of approval withdrew a dusty bottle. "Looks like you're in luck." He reached farther into the recesses of the cabinet, came up with a couple of glasses and after giving them each a swipe with the tail of his shirt, poured two healthy shots. "I could get ice from the kitchen."

"Waste of time. Unless you want it."

Matt's smile was a slow grin. "I think I'm man enough to handle warm liquor."

"Figured as much."

Thorne took the drink Matt offered and clicked the rim of his glass to his brother's. "To Randi."

"Yep."

Thorne tossed back his drink, unwinding a bit as the aged liquor splashed against the back of his throat then burned a fiery path to his stomach. He rotated his neck, trying to relieve the kinks in his neck. "Okay, so shoot," he said, as Matt lit tinder-dry kindling already stacked in the grate. "What the hell's going on?"

"Wish I knew. Near as the police can tell, Randi was involved in a single-car accident up in Glacier Park. No one knows for sure what happened and the cops are still lookin' into it, but, from what anyone can piece together, she was alone and driving and probably hit ice, or swerved to miss something—who the hell knows what, a deer maybe, your guess is as good as mine. The upshot is that she lost control and drove over the side of the road. The truck rolled down an embankment and—'' he studied the depths of his glass ''—she and the baby are lucky to be alive.''

Thorne's jaw tightened. ''Who found her?''

''Passersby—Good Samaritans who called the local sheriff's department.''

''You got their names?''

Matt reached into his back pocket and withdrew a piece of paper that he handed to Thorne. ''Jed and Bill Swanson. Brothers who were on their way home from a hunting trip. The deputy's name is on there, too.''

He read the list of names and numbers, his eyes lingering for a second when he came to Dr. Nicole Stevenson.

''I figured we should keep a list of everyone involved.''

''Good idea.'' Thorne tucked the piece of paper into his pocket. ''So do you have any idea what Randi was doing at Glacier or anywhere around here for that matter? The last I heard she was in Seattle. What about her job? Or the father of the baby?''

Matt finished his drink. ''Don't know a damned thing,'' he admitted.

''Well, that's gotta change. The three of us—Slade, you and I—we've got to find out what's going on.''

''Fine with me.'' Matt's determined gaze held his brother's.

''We'll start tonight.'' The gears were already turning in Thorne's mind. ''As soon as Slade gets in, we'll start making plans. But first things first.''

''Randi and the baby's health,'' Matt guessed.

''Yep. We can start digging around in her private

life as much as we want, but it doesn't mean a damned thing if she or the baby don't pull through.''

"They will.'' Matt was cocksure as the front door banged open and Slade appeared.

"Thanks for all the help,'' the youngest brother grumbled as he marched into the room smelling of horses and smoke. He found a glass and poured himself a stiff shot.

"You managed,'' Matt guessed.

Thorne rolled up his sleeves. "Why are you so sure that Randi and her boy will be okay?''

One side of Matt's mouth lifted. "Because they're McCaffertys, Thorne. Just like us—too ornery not to pull through.''

But Thorne wasn't convinced.

Chapter Four

"**D**on't want to dance," Molly insisted as Nicole shepherded both her daughters from the preschool and into the SUV. The rain had stopped in the night and an October sun peered through high, thin clouds.

"Why not?"

"Don't like it." Molly climbed into her car seat and started hooking the straps together while Mindy waited for her mother to snap her into place.

"Next year you can play soccer and we've got swim lessons in the spring. Until then, I think we'll stick with dance. I already paid for the lessons and they won't hurt you."

"I like to dance," Mindy said, casting her more outspoken sibling a look of pure piety. "I like Miss Palmer."

"I *hate* Miss Palmer." Molly crossed her chubby

arms over her chest and glowered at the back of the passenger seat as Nicole slid behind the steering wheel.

"It's not nice to hate." Mindy lifted her eyebrows imperiously and glanced knowingly at her mother. The angel, making sure Nicole knew that Molly was being the embodiment of evil.

"*Hate*'s a pretty strong word," Nicole said and started the SUV. The engine fired on the first try. "Atta girl," she added and Mindy nodded, thinking her mother was praising her. Dark curls bounced around her head as she sent her twin a holier-than-thou look of supreme patience.

"Quit that! Mommy, she's *looking* at me."

"It's okay."

"I want ice cream," Molly insisted.

"Right after dance."

"I *hate* dance."

"I know, I know, we've been over this before," Nicole said adjusting the heat and defrost. Sun or no sun, the air was still cold. She drove over a small bridge and past a strip mall to the older side of town where an old brick grade school had been converted into artists' quarters. She parked, took the girls inside, and rather than stay and watch them go through their routine, she drove to the service station where the mechanic looked under the hood of the SUV, lifted his grimy hat and scratched his head.

"Beats me," he admitted, shifting a toothpick from one side of his mouth to the other. An elderly man with a barrel body and silver beard stubble, he frowned and wiped the oil from his hands. "Seems to be working just fine. Why don't you bring it in next week and leave it—can you? We'll run diagnostics on it.''

She made an appointment, mentally crossed her fingers, rounded up the girls and managed to stop at the grocery store and ice-cream parlor before they had a total meltdown.

"Why doesn't Daddy live with us?" Mindy asked as they pulled into the driveway of their house.

Nicole parked and pocketed her keys. "Because Mommy and Daddy are divorced, you know that. Come on, let's get out of the car."

"And Daddy lives far away," Molly said, drips of bubble-gum ice cream falling from her chin.

"He don't come and see us. Bobbi Martin's daddy comes and visits her."

"Would you like for your father to visit?" Nicole had opened the back door and was unsnapping the straps to Mindy's car seat.

"Yeth."

"Nope." Molly shook her head. "He don't like us."

"Oh, Molly—" Nicole was about to argue and then saw no reason to defend Paul. He'd had no interest in the twins since the divorce. Sending Nicole child support payments seemed to fulfill all his requirements as a father; at least in his opinion. "You just don't know your father."

"Is he going to come see us?" Mindy asked, her eyes bright, her ice-cream cone forgotten. The single scoop of cookies-n-cream was melting into her fingers.

"I don't know. He doesn't have any plans to, not yet. But, if you like, I could call him."

"Call him!" Mindy swiped at the top of her cone with her tongue.

"He won't come." Molly didn't seem upset about it; she was just stating a fact. "You can have the rest," she said, handing her mother the cone and bolting from the rig. She tore off across the wet grass to the swing set.

"Can't you undo this yourself?" Nicole asked lifting the safety bar of the car seat.

"You do it." Mindy smiled impishly, then, still clutching her cone, slid out of the car.

You're spoiling her, Nicole told herself as she juggled the grocery sacks and carried them into the house. *You're spoiling them both, trying to be father and mother, feeling sorry for them because, they, like you, are growing up without their father.*

Was it her fault? She had a lot of reasons for moving away from San Francisco, for wanting to start over. But maybe in so doing, she was robbing her daughters of a vital part of their lives, of the chance to know the man who'd sired them.

Not that he'd shown any interest when they still lived in the city. He'd never seen the girls for more than a couple of hours at a time and his new wife had been pretty clear that she saw his twins as "baggage" she didn't want or need.

So Nicole wasn't going to beat herself up about it. The twins were doing fine. Just fine.

Patches, who had been washing his face on the windowsill, hopped lithely to the floor. "Naughty boy," Nicole whispered, but added some dry food to his dish, unpacked the groceries and watched her girls through the back window. They were playing on the teeter-totter, laughing in the crisp air as clouds began to gather again. Nicole pressed the play button on the answering machine.

The first voice she heard was Thorne McCafferty's.

"Hi. It's Thorne. Call me." He rattled off his phone number and Nicole's stomach did a flip at the sound of it. Why he got to her after all these years she didn't understand, but he did. There was no doubt about it. She knew that he'd been her first love, but it had been years, *years* since then. So why did he still affect her? She glanced to the windowsill where she'd placed the bud vase with its single white rose— a peace offering, nothing more.

Sighing, she wished she understood why she couldn't shake Thorne from her thoughts. She wasn't a lonely woman. She wasn't a needy woman. She *didn't* want a man in her life—at least not yet. So why was it that every time she heard his voice those old memories that she'd tucked away escaped to run and play havoc through her mind?

"Because you're an idiot," she said and finished unloading the car. She remembered seeing him for the first time, the summer before her senior year in high school. He'd been alone, dusk was settling, the sky still glowing pink over the western hills, the first stars beginning to sparkle in the night. The heat of the day hung heavy in the air with only a breath of a breeze to lift her hair or brush her cheeks. She was sitting on a blanket, alone, her best friend having ditched her at the last minute to be with her boyfriend and suddenly Thorne had appeared, tall, strapping, wearing a T-shirt that stretched over his shoulders and faded jeans that hung low on his hips.

"Is this spot taken?" he'd asked and she hadn't responded, thinking he had to be talking to someone else.

"Excuse me," he'd said again and she'd twisted her face up to stare into intense gray eyes that took hold of her and wouldn't let go. "Would it be all right if I sat here?"

She couldn't believe her ears. There were dozens of blankets tossed upon the bent grass of the hillside, hundreds of people gathered and picnicking as they waited for the show. And he wanted to sit *here?* Next to her? "Oh, well...sure," she'd managed to reply, feeling like an utter fool, her face burning with embarrassment.

He'd taken a spot next to her on her blanket, his arms draped over half-bent knees, his spine curved, his body so close to hers she could smell some kind of cologne or soap, barely an inch between his shoulder and hers. Suddenly she found it impossible to breathe. "Thanks," he said, his voice low, his smile a flash of white against a strong, beard-shadowed chin. "I'm Thorne. McCafferty."

She'd recognized the name, of course, had heard the rumors and gossip swirling about his family. She had even met his younger brothers upon an occasion or two, but she'd never been face-to-face with the oldest McCafferty son. Never in her life had she felt the wild drumming of her heart just because a man—and that was it, he wasn't a boy—was regarding her with assessing steely eyes.

Five or six years older than she, he seemed light-years ahead of her in sophistication. He'd been off to college somewhere on the East Coast, she thought, an

Ivy League school, though she couldn't really remember which one.

"I imagine you do have a name." His lips twitched and she felt even a bigger fool.

"Oh...yes. I'm Nicole Sanders." She started to offer him her hand, then let it drop.

"Is that what you go by? Nicole?"

"Yeah." She swallowed hard and glanced away. Clearing her throat she nodded. "Sometimes Nikki." She felt like a little girl in her ponytail and cutoff jeans and sleeveless blouse with the shirttails tied around her waist.

"Nikki, I like that." Plucking a long piece of dry grass from the hillside he shoved it into his mouth and as Nicole surreptitiously watched, he moved it from one sexy corner to the other. And he was sexy. More purely male and raw than any boy she'd ever been with. "You live around here?"

"Yeah. In town. Alder Street."

"I'll remember that," he promised and her silly heart took flight. "Alder."

Dear God, she thought she'd die. Right then and there. He winked at her, stretched out and leaned back on his elbows while taking in the back of her head and the darkening heavens.

As the fireworks had started that night, bursting in the sky in brilliant flashes of green, yellow and blue, Nicole Frances Sanders spent the evening in exquisite teenage torment and, without a thought to the consequences, began to fall in love.

It seemed eons ago—a magical point in time that was long past. But, like it or not, even now, while standing in her cozy little kitchen, she felt the tingle of excitement, the lilt, she'd always experienced when she'd been with Thorne.

"Don't go there," she warned herself, her hands gripping the edge of the counter so hard her fingers ached. "That was a long, long time ago." A time Thorne, no doubt, didn't remember.

She waited until she'd fed and bathed the girls, read them stories, and then, dreading talking to him, punched out the number for the Flying M Ranch.

Thorne picked up on the second ring. "Flying M. Thorne McCafferty."

"Hi, it's Nicole. You called?" she asked while the twins ran pell-mell through the house.

"Yeah. I thought we should get together."

She nearly dropped the phone. "Get together? For?"

"Dinner."

A *date?* He was asking her out? Her heart began to thud and in the peripheral vision she saw the rose with its soft white petals beginning to open. "Was there a reason?"

"More than one, actually. I want to talk to you about Randi and the baby, of course. Their treatment, what happens if we can't find the baby's father, convalescent care and rehabilitation when Randi's finally released. That kind of thing."

"Oh." She felt strangely deflated. "Sure, I suppose, but her doctors will go over all this with you."

"But they're not you." His voice was low and her pulse elevated again.

"They're professionals."

"But I don't know them. I don't trust them."

"And you trust me?" she said, unable to stop herself.

"Yes."

The twins roared into the room. "Mommy, Mommy—she hit me!" Molly cried, outraged, while Mindy, eyes round, shook her head solemnly.

"Not me."

"Yes, she did."

"You hit me first." Molly began to wail.

"Thorne, would you excuse me. My daughters are in the middle of their own little war."

"Oh, I didn't realize." He paused for a second as she bent on one knee, stretching the phone cord and giving Molly a hug. "I didn't know you had children."

"Two girls, dynamos. I'm divorced," she added quickly. "Nearly two years now."

Was there a sigh of relief on his end of the conversation, or did she imagine it over Molly's sobs?

"I'll talk to you later," he said.

"Yes. Do." She hung up and threw her arms around both girls, but her thoughts were already rushing forward to thoughts of Thorne and being alone with him. She couldn't do it. Even though he'd tried to apologize for leaving her and she'd spent years fantasizing about just such a scenario, she wouldn't risk being with him again. It wasn't just herself and her heart she had to worry about now, she had the girls to consider. And yet…a part of her would love to see him again, to smile into his eyes, to kiss him… She pulled herself up short. What was she thinking? The kiss in the parking lot had been passionate, wild and evoked memories of their lovemaking so long ago, but it was the kiss on her cheek that had really gotten to her, the soft featherlike caress of his lips against her skin that made her want more.

"Stop it," she told herself.

"Stop what?" Mindy looked at her mother with wounded, teary eyes. "I didn't do it!"

"I know, sweetie, I know," Nicole said, determined not to let Thorne McCafferty bulldoze his way into her life...or her heart.

Thorne walked into the barn and shoved thoughts of Nicole out of his mind. He had too many other problems, pressing issues to deal with. Besides Randi's and the baby's health, there were questions about her accident and, of course, the ever present responsibilities he'd left behind in Denver—hundreds of miles away but still requiring his attention.

The smells of fresh hay, dusty hides and oiled leather brought back memories of his youth—memories he'd pushed aside long ago. As the first few drops of rain began to pepper the tin roof, Slade was tossing hay bales down from the loft above. Matt carried the bales by their string to the appropriate mangers, then deftly sliced the twine with his jackknife. Thorne grabbed a pitchfork and, as he had every winter day in his youth, began shaking loose hay into the manger.

The cattle were inside lowing and shifting, edging toward the piles of feed. Red, dun, black and gray, their coats were thick with the coming of winter, covered with dust and splattered with mud.

After a day of being on the phone, the physical labor felt good and eased some of the tension from muscles that had been cramped in his father's desk chair. Thorne had called Nicole, his office in Denver, several clients and potential business partners, as well as local retailers as he needed equipment to set up a temporary office here at the ranch. But that had just been the beginning; the rest of the day he'd spent at the hospital, talking with doctors or searching for clues as to what had happened to his sister.

For the most part, he'd come up dry. "So no one's figured out why Randi was back in Montana?" he said, tossing a forkful of hay into the manger. A white-faced heifer plunged her broad nose into the hay.

"I called around this afternoon while you were at the hospital." The three brothers had visited their sister individually and checked in on their new nephew. Thorne had hoped to run into Nicole. He hadn't.

"What did you find out?"

"Diddly-squat." Another bale dropped from above. Slade swung down as well, landing next to Thorne and wincing at the jolt in his bad leg. His limp was still as noticeable as the red line that ran from his temple to his chin, compliments of a skiing accident that had nearly taken his life, though the scars on the outside of his face were far less damaging than those that, Thorne imagined, cut through his soul. "I talked to several people at the *Seattle Clarion* where she wrote her column, whatever the hell it is." Slade yanked a pitchfork from its resting place on the wall.

"Advice to the lovelorn," Thorne supplied. Drops of frigid rain drizzled down the small windows and a wind, screaming of winter, tore through the valley.

"It's a lot more than that," Matt said defensively. "It's general advice to single people. Things like legal issues, divorce settlements, raising kids alone, dealing with grief and new relationships, juggling time around career and kids, budgeting…hell, I don't know."

"Sounds like you do," Thorne said, realizing that Matt had maintained a stronger relationship with their half sister than he had. But then that hadn't been difficult.

"I take a paper that prints her column. It's been syndicated, y'know. Picked up by a few independents as far away as Chicago."

"Is that right?" Thorne felt a sharp jab of guilt. What did he know about his sister? Not much.

"Yeah, she adds her own touch—her quirky humor—and it sells."

"Since when did she become an expert?" Slade wanted to know.

"Beats me." Matt scratched the stubble on his chin. "Looks like she could've used some pearls of wisdom herself."

Thorne kicked at a bale, causing it to split open. Why hadn't Randi come to him, explained about the baby, confided in him if her life wasn't going well? His back teeth ground together and he reminded himself that maybe she didn't know things weren't on track, maybe this baby was planned. "Okay, so what else did you find out?" he asked, refusing to wallow in a sea of guilt.

Slade lifted a shoulder. "Not a hell of a lot. Her co-workers, of course, all figured out she was pregnant. She couldn't really hide it. But none of them admitted to knowing the father's name.''

"You think they're lying?" Thorne asked.

"Not that I could tell."

"Great."

"No one even thinks she was dating anyone seriously."

"Looks serious enough to me," Matt grumbled.

Slade reached across the manger and pushed one cow's white face to the side so a smaller animal could wedge her nose into the hay. "Move, there," he commanded, though the beast didn't so much as flick her ears. Wiping his hand on the bleached denim of his jeans, he said, "Randi's editor, Bill Withers, said that she'd planned to take a three-month maternity leave, but he'd assumed she'd stay in town, because she told him that as soon as she was on her feet and she and the baby were settled in, she was going to work out of her condominium. She had enough columns written ahead that they'll run for a few weeks. Then, she'd be back at it again, though she didn't plan to start going into the office until after the first of the year."

"So there was no trouble at work?"

"None that anyone is saying, but I get the feeling that there was more going on than anyone's willing to admit."

"Par for the course. Reporters, they're always ready to snoop into anyone else's business—they've already been calling here, you know. But ask them about what they know and all of a sudden the First Amendment becomes the Bible." Matt snorted and picked up the used strands of baling twine. "Does anyone at her office know anything about her accident?''

''Nope.'' Slade dusted his hands. ''They were shocked. Especially the ones she was supposedly closest to. Sarah Peeples, who writes movie reviews gasped and nearly fell through the floor, from the sound of her end of the conversation. She couldn't believe that Randi was in the hospital and Dave Delacroix, he's a guy who writes a sports column for the paper, thought I was playing some kind of practical joke. Then once he figured out I was on the level, he got angry. Demanded answers. So, basically, I drew blanks.''

''It's a start,'' Thorne said as they finished up. The wheels had been turning in his mind from the moment he'd heard about Randi's accident; now it was time to put some kind of plan into action. Slade forked the last wisps of hay into the manger. ''I'll catch up with you,'' he said as he traded his pitchfork for a broom. ''Pour me a drink.''

''Will do.'' Thorne followed Matt outside and dashed through rain cold enough that he knew winter was in the air.

Once in the house again, Matt built another fire from last night's embers and Thorne poured them each a drink. As they waited for Slade, they sipped their father's Scotch and worried aloud about their headstrong sister and wondering how they would take care of a newborn.

''The problem is, none of us know much about Randi's life,'' Thorne said as he capped the bottle.

''I think that's the way she wanted it. We can beat ourselves up one side and down the other for not being a part of her life, but that was Randi's choice. Remember?''

How could he forget? At their father's funeral in May, Randi had been inconsolable, refusing any outward show of emotion from her brothers, preferring to stand in an oversize, gauzy black dress apart from the rest of the family, while a young preacher, who knew very little of the man in the coffin prayed solemnly. Most of the townspeople of Grand Hope came to the service to pay their respects.

She had to have been four months pregnant at the time. Thorne would never have guessed as they paid their last respects on the hillside. But then he'd been lost in his own black thoughts, the ring his father had given him the summer before hidden deep in his pocket.

John Randall hadn't been a churchgoing man. Under the circumstances, the young minister whose eulogy had been from notes he'd taken the day earlier, had done a decent enough job asking that the blackheart's soul be accepted into heaven. Thorne wasn't certain God had made such a huge exception.

''Randi's kept her life pretty private.''

''Haven't we all?'' Matt remarked.

''Maybe it's time to change all that.'' Thorne ran a hand through the thin layer of dust that had collected on the mantel.

''Agreed.'' Matt lifted his glass and nodded.

The front door banged open. A gust of cold wind blew through the hallway and Slade, wiping the rain from his face, hitched himself into the living room. He shrugged out of his jacket and tossed it over the back of the couch.

"Any word on Randi?" Making his way across the braided rug, Slade found an old-fashioned glass in the cupboard and without much fanfare, poured himself a long drink from the rapidly diminishing bottle of Scotch.

"Not yet. But I'll check the answering machine." Matt crossed the room and disappeared down the hallway leading to the den.

"She'd better pull out of this," Slade said, as if to himself. The youngest of the three brothers, Slade was also the wildest. He'd left a trail of broken hearts from Mexico to Canada, if rumors were to be believed and never had really settled down. While Matt had his own ranch, a small spread near the Idaho border, Slade had put down no roots and probably never would. He'd done everything from race cars, to ride rodeo, and do stunt work in films. The scar running down one side of his face was testament to his hard, reckless lifestyle and Thorne had, at times, wondered if the youngest McCafferty son harbored some kind of death wish.

Slade stood in front of the fire and warmed the backs of his legs. "What're we gonna do about the baby?"

"We take care of him until Randi's able."

"Then we'd better get this place ready," Slade observed.

"The orthopedist called earlier," Matt said, entering the room. "As soon as some of the swelling has gone down and Randi's out of critical condition, he'll take care of her leg."

"Good. I put a call in to Nicole. I want to meet

with her so that she can tell me about Randi's doctors and her prognosis, rehab, that sort of thing.''

"Nicole?'' Matt replied, his eyes narrowing as if struck by a sudden memory. ''You know she mentioned that you knew each other, but I'd forgotten that you were an item.''

"It was only a few weeks,'' Thorne clarified.

Slade rubbed the back of his neck. ''I hardly remember it.''

"Because you were off racing cars and chasing women on the stock car circuit,'' Matt said. ''You weren't around much when Thorne got out of college and was heading to law school. It was that summer, right?''

"Part of the summer.''

Slade shook his head. ''Let me guess, you dumped her for some other long-legged plaything.''

"There was no other woman,'' Thorne snapped, surprised at the anger surging through his blood.

"No, you just had to go out and prove to Dad and God and anyone else who would listen that you could make it on your own without J. Randall's help.''

"It was a long time ago,'' Thorne muttered. ''Right now we've got to concentrate on Randi.''

"And that's why you called Dr. Stevenson?'' Obviously Matt wasn't buying it.

"Of course.'' Thorne sat on the arm of the leather couch and knew he was lying, not only to his brothers but to himself. It was more than just wanting to discuss Randi's condition with her; he wanted to see Nicole again, be with her. The strange part of it was, ever since seeing her again, he wanted to see more of her. ''Now, listen,'' he said to his brothers. ''Something we'll have to deal with and pronto is finding out who the father is.''

"That's gonna be tough considerin' Randi's condition." Slade rested a shoulder against the mantel and folded his arms over his chest. "Just how long you plannin' on stickin' around, city boy?"

"As long as it takes."

"Aren't there some big deals in Denver and Laramie and wherever the hell else you own property— things you need to oversee?"

Thorne resisted being baited and managed a guarded grin, the kind Slade so often gave the rest of the world. "I can oversee them from here."

"How?"

"By the fine art of telecommunication. I'll set up a fax, modem, Internet connection, cell phone and computer in the den."

Matt rubbed his chin. "Thought you hated it here. Except for a few times like that summer after you graduated from college you've avoided this ranch like the plague. Ever since Dad and Mom split, you've spent as little time here as possible."

Thorne couldn't argue the fact. "Randi needs me— us."

Matt added wood to the fire and switched on a lamp. "Okay, I think we need a game plan," Thorne said.

"Let me guess, you'll be the quarterback, just like in high school," Slade said.

Thorne's temper snapped. "Let's just work together, okay? It's not about calling the shots so much as getting the job done."

"Okay." Matt nodded. "I'll be in charge of the

ranch. I've already talked to a couple of guys who will help out.''

Slade walked to the couch and picked up his jacket. "Good enough. Matt should run the place, he's used to it and I'll pitch in if we need an extra hand. Thorne, why don't you give Juanita a call? Maybe she can help with the baby. She's had some experience raising McCaffertys, after all, she helped Dad with us.''

"Good idea, as we'll need round-the-clock help," Thorne decided.

"We'll get it. Now, the way I think I can help best is by concentrating on finding out all I can about what was going on in our sister's life, especially in the past year or so. I have a friend who's a private investigator. For the right price, he'll help us out," Slade said.

"Is he any good?" Thorne asked.

Slade's expression turned dark. "If anyone can find out what's going on, it'll be Kurt Striker. I'd bet my life on it."

"You're sure?"

Slade's gaze could've cut through steel. "I said, I'd bet my life on it. I meant that. Literally.''

"Call him," Thorne said, persuaded by his usually cynical brother's conviction.

"Already have."

Thorne was surprised that Slade had already started the ball rolling. "I want to talk to him."

"You will."

"I'll keep on top of the doctors at the hospital," Thorne said. "I'll can do most of my business here by phone, fax and e-mail, so I won't have to go back to Denver for a while.''

Matt held his gaze for a long second and for the first time in his life Thorne realized that his middle brother didn't approve of his lifestyle. Not that it really mattered. "Then let's just get through this," Matt finally said, as if he suddenly trusted Thorne again, as he had a long time before.

"We will."

"As long as Randi cooperates," Slade said.

"She's a fighter." Thorne's reaction was swift and he recognized the irony of his words. Phrases such as *she's really strong, she'll make it,* or *she's too ornery to die,* or *she's a fighter,* were hollow words, expressed by people who usually doubted their meaning. They were uttered to chase away the person's own fears.

"Look, I'm going to take inventory of the feed," Matt said.

"I'll check the gas pump, see what's in the tank." Slade snagged his jacket with one finger and the two younger brothers headed for the front door.

Thorne watched them through the window. Slade paused to light a cigarette on the porch while Matt jogged across the lot, disappearing into the barn again.

As kids they'd been through a lot together; depended upon each other, but as men, they'd gone about their own lives. Thorne had become the businessman, first law school and a stint with a firm before branching out on his own. His father had been right. He'd wanted to prove himself and the measure of a man's success, he'd always thought, was the size of his bank account.

For the first time in his life he wondered if he'd

been wrong. Thinking of Randi battling death and her newborn son just starting his life gave him pause as he walked down the hallway where family portraits graced the walls. There were pictures of his father and mother, his stepmother and all four McCafferty children. Thorne in his high school football uniform and his graduation cap and gown, Matt riding a bucking bronco in a local rodeo, Slade skiing down a steep mountain and Randi in her prom dress, standing next to some boy Thorne couldn't begin to name. He stopped, touched that framed photo and silently vowed that he'd do anything, *anything* to make sure she was healthy again. He'd heat a cup of coffee, then call Nicole. She might have more news on his sister. That was the only reason he was calling her, he reminded himself as he walked into the kitchen and snapped on the lights. From the corner of his eye, he caught sight of his reflection in the windows. For a split second he imagined a mite of a woman with wide gold eyes and a fleeting smile at his side, then pulled himself up short.

What was he thinking? Nicole was Randi's ER admitting physician and that was it. Nothing more. Yet, ever since he'd first seen her in her office at the hospital, her heels propped on her desk, and her chair leaned back as she cradled the phone between her ear and shoulder, he hadn't been able to force her from his mind. It hadn't helped that when he'd caught up with her in the parking lot, he'd seen her not as Randi's doctor, but as a woman—a beautiful, bright and articulate woman. He hadn't been able to stop himself from kissing her and he'd been thinking about it off and on ever since. Nicole Sanders Stevenson

was all grown-up, educated and self-confident—more
intriguing now then she had been as a girl of seventeen. Despite her small stature she was a force to be
reckoned with—way too much trouble for any man.

And yet...

The wall phone jangled. Snapped out of the ridiculous path of his thoughts, he grabbed the receiver on
the second ring. "McCafferty ranch," he said.
"Thorne McCafferty."

"So you are there!" a sharp female voice accused,
and Thorne envisioned Annette's pretty face in a
scowl. He'd dated her for a few months, but had never
really connected with her. "What in the world happened? We were supposed to meet the mayor last
night!" Annette's tone brought him up sharp and he
gave himself a quick mental shake. He'd never called
her. Never once thought of her after leaving his office
yesterday.

"There was a family emergency."

"So you couldn't pick up a phone? You have a
cell phone and you're on one right now...oh, listen,
I don't mean to go off on you." She took in a deep,
audible breath. "Your secretary told me that your half
sister was in some kind of wreck and I'm sorry for
her, I really am. I hope she's okay...?"

"She's in a coma."

"Oh, God." There was another long, weighty
pause. "Well, I, um, understand, I really do. Dear
Lord, how awful. I know you had to get back there
in a hurry, Thorne. That's understandable and I made
your apologies to my father and the mayor, but it
seems to me that you could have called me yourself."

"I should have."

"Yeah...oh, well." She sighed. "Dad was disappointed."

"Was he?" Thorne drawled, imagining Kent Williams's reaction. The shrewd old man was probably in a stew as he'd wanted to invest with Thorne and was hoping they could cozy up with members of the city council and get an edge on a zoning ordinance that was up for review. "Thanks for giving him my apologies. You didn't have to do that. I would have called him."

"And me, would you have called me?"

"Yes."

"Eventually."

"Right." No reason to lie. "Eventually."

"Oh, Thorne." She let out a world-weary sigh and some of the shrewishness in her voice disappeared. "I miss you."

Did she? He doubted it and their relationship had always left him feeling alone. "It looks like I'm going to be in Montana a while."

"Oh." There was hesitation in her voice. "How long?"

"A few weeks, maybe months. It all depends on Randi."

"But what about your work?"

"What about it?"

"It's—it's your life."

Was my life, he wanted to say. Instead, added, "Things have changed."

"Have they?" Silent accusations sizzled over the wires.

"Afraid so."

"What does that mean?" But she knew. It was

obvious. "You know, there are other men who are interested in me. I've put them on hold because of you."

"I'm sorry."

She waited and the silence ticked between them. "So, what're you telling me, Thorne?" she asked. "That it's over? Just like that? Because your sister is in the hospital?"

"No, Annette," he admitted, "it's not because of Randi. You and I both know that this wasn't going anywhere. I was up front about that at the beginning."

"I thought you'd change your mind."

"It didn't happen."

"So I should start seeing other men."

"It wouldn't be a bad idea."

"Okay." Again a frosty pause. "I'll think about it," she said.

"Do."

"And you, too, Thorne," she said with a renewed amount of spunk. "You think about what you're giving up." She hung up with a click and he replaced the receiver slowly, wondering why he didn't feel any sense of loss. But then he never had; not with any woman. Not even with Nikki way back when, and she'd been the most difficult. But he hadn't trusted her with his heart and when it came time to take off for law school, he'd left Grand Hope, his family and Nicole Sanders and never once looked back. Until now. While away at school, whenever he'd thought of her, which was often at first, he steadfastly turned his mind to other things. Eventually he'd quit thinking about her altogether and he'd lived by the axiom that women weren't a priority in his life.

But now, as he stared out the window into the dark, wet night, he felt a change inside him, a new kind of need. He reached for the phone as it rang again sharply.

Annette. He should have known she wouldn't give up without a fight.

"Hello," he said, as the receiver reached his ear.

"Thorne? This is Nicole." Her voice was cold and professional.

He knew in a heartbeat that Randi's condition had worsened. Fear clutched his heart and for the first time in his life he felt absolutely helpless. Oh, God. "It's my sister," he stated.

"No. Randi's still stable, but I just got a call from the hospital because they couldn't get through to you—your line was busy." Nicole hesitated a beat and before she got the words out, Thorne experienced an anguish the like of which he'd never felt before. He sagged against the wall as she said, "It's the baby."

Chapter Five

"What about him?" Thorne clutched the receiver in a death grip. His heart thudded in dread. For the love of Mike, how could one little baby, Randi's son whom he'd never even held, make such a difference in his life?

He heard the back door open and Matt, unbuttoning his sheepskin jacket, strode in. "Slade's still—"

Thorne silenced his brother with a killing glance and a finger to his lips.

"What about the baby?" he repeated, bracing himself and he saw Matt's dark complexion pale.

"He's lethargic, experiencing feeding problems and respiratory distress, his abdomen is distended, his temp has spiked—"

"Just cut to the chase, Nicole. What's he got? What went wrong?" Thorne was pacing now, stretching the telephone cord as Matt's eyes followed his every move.

Nicole hesitated a beat and Thorne found it hard to breathe. "Dr. Arnold thinks the baby might have bacterial meningitis. He's going to call you later and—"

"Meningitis?" Thorne repeated.

"No way!" Matt broke his silence.

"How the hell did that happen?"

"When Randi came into the hospital, her membranes had already ruptured—"

"What? Ruptured?"

Matt wore under his breath, then looked up, his gaze locking with that of his older brother. "Let's go," Matt said. "Right now. To the damned hospital!" Thorne cut him off with a quick shake of his head. He had to concentrate.

Nicole was talking again—her voice calm, though he sensed an urgency to her. "Her water had broken in the accident and there's a chance that there was contamination, the baby was exposed to some source of bacteria."

"This Dr. Arnold? Is he there? At the hospital now?"

"Yes. He'll call you with more information—"

"We're on our way."

"I'll meet you there," she said as he slammed the receiver down.

"What the hell's going on?" Matt demanded.

"The baby's in trouble. It doesn't sound good." Thorne was already striding to the front hall where he yanked his coat from a hook and shoved his arms down the sleeves. Matt was right on his heels. The two men half ran to Thorne's truck, but before he climbed into the passenger side, Matt said, "Wait a minute, I'd better tell Slade that we're on our way to the hospital—"

"Make it fast," Thorne ordered, but Matt was already running toward the barn. He disappeared inside. Thorne jabbed his key into the ignition, the truck roared to life and he glared at the barn, willing his brother to return.

Less than a minute later Matt, head ducked, holding on to the brim of his Stetson, dashed through the rain. Thorne was already throwing the pickup into gear by the time Matt opened the door and slid inside.

"He's gonna follow us."

"Good."

Thorne stepped hard on the accelerator, though he didn't know why. The urge to get to the hospital, to do *something* pounded through him. What had gone wrong?

Rain poured from the sky and the twin ruts of the lane glistened in the glow of the headlights as water spun beneath the tires.

"Okay, now what happened?" Matt demanded, his face tense in the dark interior.

"Something went wrong."

"What?"

"Everything." Thorne squinted against oncoming headlights, shifted down and turned onto the main road cutting through the pine-forested canyons and rolling acres of farmland surrounding the Flying M. In clipped words, Thorne repeated his conversation with Nicole.

Matt's jaw clenched. "Why was Nicole the one who called? Why not the pediatrician?"

"He couldn't get through, but I'll have more phone lines installed. Tomorrow. And I'd asked Nicole to phone me if there was any change. She said Dr. Arnold would call us, but I'm not going to hang around and wait. I want answers and I want them now."

The ranch was nearly twenty miles from town. Thorne pushed the speed limit and the truck's tires sang against the wet pavement.

They arrived at the hospital in record time. Thorne was out of the truck like a shot. Matt kept up with him, stride for stride. They sprinted across the dark parking lot, flew through the automatic doors of the lobby, then took the stairs two at a time to the second floor.

This time, Thorne didn't allow any nurse to tell him what to do. The poor woman, a slight blonde with a tentative smile tried to ward them off. "Excuse me, you can't come in here," she said, pointing to a sign that read Authorized Personnel Only.

"Where's the McCafferty baby?" Thorne demanded.

"Who are you?"

"I'm the baby's uncle and so is he," Matt said, hooking a thumb toward Thorne. "We're Randi McCafferty's brothers."

"The only family the baby has right now," Thorne explained, "as our sister is in Intensive Care and we haven't located the child's father." That wasn't a lie. Not really. He just didn't bother to add that they had no idea who the father was. Slicing Matt a look warning him not to elaborate, Thorne continued. "I want to see my nephew."

"He's in his crib," the nurse said patiently. "And

he's being monitored closely.'' Her lips pursed and she motioned toward the glassed-in room where the baby, lying seemingly peacefully under a warm lamp, with a monitor strapped to him, was sleeping. Tubes were inserted into his small body and he breathed with his tiny mouth open. Another nurse hovered near his plastic bed. The blonde nurse continued, ''Dr. Arnold has seen him and should be right back—oh, here he is now.'' She was obviously relieved to pass the responsibility of dealing with Thorne and Matt to a small man with wire-rimmed glasses, slightly stooped shoulders and a ring of wild white hair.

''Dr. Arnold?'' Thorne asked, pinning the shorter man with his gaze.

''Yes.''

''I'm Thorne McCafferty. This is my brother, Matt. The baby's mother is our sister. What the hell's going on?''

''That's what we're trying to find out,'' Dr. Arnold said calmly, obviously not offended by Thorne's sharp words and demanding attitude. ''The baby's suffering from bacterial meningitis, probably contracted at the site of the accident as your sister's amniotic sac had already ruptured.'' Thorne's chest tightened. He felt a muscle in his jaw work as the doctor explained in finer detail what Nicole had already told him on the phone. Slade, white-faced, jaw set, fists coiled, arrived and was introduced quickly and brought up to speed.

''So how dangerous is this?'' Thorne demanded.

''Very.'' The doctor was solemn. ''We're a small hospital but luckily, we've got a state-of-the-art intensive pediatric unit.''

Matt got straight to the point. "Is the baby going to make it?"

"I wish I could tell you that he's out of the woods, but I can't." The doctor's eyes, behind his glasses, were solemn. "The mortality rate for this kind of meningitis is high, somewhere between twenty to fifty percent—"

"Oh, God," Matt whispered.

"However, your nephew's survival chances are good here because of the staff and equipment. Already the baby's on antibiotic therapy and a mechanical ventilator along with compulsive fluid management."

"What?"

"An IV to minimize the effects of cerebral edema. Even if the baby is to survive, there's a chance that he might be deaf, blind or have some retardation."

"Damn," Slade mumbled and ran a hand over his chin and was suddenly pale as death, his scar more visible.

Thorne was thunderstruck. He stared at Randi's baby and felt, for the first time in his life, impotent. Frustration burned through his bloodstream.

"Isn't there anything else you can do?" Matt asked, lines of worry sketching his brow.

"There must be," Thorne added.

"Believe me, we're doing everything possible." Dr. Arnold's voice was steady.

"If there's anything he needs, anything at all—equipment, specialists, whatever—we'll pay for it." Thorne was adamant. "Money isn't an issue here."

The doctor's lips pulled together just a fraction. His spine seemed to stiffen and his voice was clipped.

"Money isn't the problem right now, Mr. Mc-
Cafferty. As I said we have the best equipment available, but this hospital is always looking for endow-
ments and benefactors. I'll see that your name is on
the list. Now, if you'll excuse me, I want to check on
my patient."

He punched a code into a keypad and the doors
marked Authorized Personnel Only opened. Dr. Arnold disappeared for an instant before he stepped into
the neonatal nursery and was visible through the thick
glass of the viewing window. Thorne's teeth
clenched, anger and impotence burned in his brain.
There had to be something he could do to help
Randi's boy. There had to be! He stared at the pediatrician hard, but if Dr. Arnold felt Thorne's eyes
upon him, he didn't so much as flinch or glance up.
Instead he focused on the baby, carefully examining
the fragile little boy who was Randi's only child—
John Randall McCafferty's sole grandchild.

"He's got to pull through," Matt said, his fists ball-
ing in determination. "If he doesn't and Randi wakes
up to find out that he didn't make it—"

"Don't say it! Don't even think it! He's gonna be
fine. He's got to!" Slade slashed Matt a harsh glance
filled with his own private hell. Not too long ago he'd
lost a girlfriend and an unborn child. "He'll make it."

"Will he?" Matt wasn't convinced. "Here? I
mean, I know this is a good hospital—the best
around—but maybe he needs specialists, the kind that
you find in bigger cities at teaching hospitals in L.A.
or Denver or Seattle."

"We'll check it out," Thorne agreed. "I'll find out
the best in the country."

"Right now it would be a mistake to move him." Nicole's voice came from somewhere down the hallway.

Thorne hadn't heard her approach but saw her reflection in the glass, a pale ghost in jeans and ski jacket, a filmy image that pulled strangely on his heartstrings. "Trust me on this one, Thorne, the baby's in good hands."

He turned and stared into a face devoid of makeup except for a bit of lipstick, her hair falling freely to her shoulders, her gold eyes quietly reassuring. She looked younger than she had before, more like the girl he remembered, the one he'd thought he'd loved, the one he'd so callously left behind. "Sorry it took me a while to get here, I had to round up a baby-sitter."

"You have a child?" Matt asked.

"Two. Twin girls. Four years old." Her serious face brightened at the mention of her daughters and Thorne tried to ignore the ridiculous spurt of jealousy that ran through his blood that another man had fathered her daughters, then he gave himself a swift mental shake. What the hell was he thinking? "And I'd trust them to Geoff—er, Dr. Arnold."

"Good enough for me," Matt allowed, though his face was still tense.

"Nothin' else we can do but have some faith in the guy," Slade agreed, then cursed softly in frustration.

"There're are always other options," Thorne disagreed.

"None better." Nicole's voice brooked no argument. Her face was a mask of certainty. She had absolute trust in this man and again, ludicrously, Thorne felt a prick of jealousy that she would have such unflagging confidence in another male. "Let me talk to Geoff and see what's up." Nicole punched a code into the door lock. "I'll just be a minute." The electronic doors opened. Nicole slipped through.

Slade shifted from one foot to the other. Scowling through the glass, he eyed the two doctors and finally said, "I think I'll go check on Randi, then head back. You can fill me in when you get home."

Matt nodded curtly. "I'll come with you." He glanced at Thorne. "I'll catch a ride back to the ranch with Slade."

"Fine," Thorne said. "Call Striker again. Tell him I want to talk to him. ASAP."

"What about?" Slade asked.

"The kid's father for starters."

"Okay, I'll try to find Kurt."

"Don't try. Do it."

Slade's eyes flared and he slanted Thorne a condescending, don't-push-me-around smile. "Don't worry, brother. I'll handle it." With that he turned and walked away.

"Hell, you can be an insufferable bastard," Matt growled. "You might be used to barking orders at your office and everyone hustles to do what you want, but back off a bit, okay? We're all in this together. Slade'll call Striker."

"Will he?" Thorne's eyes narrowed. "It seems to me he's made a lot of promises in his life that he somehow managed to forget."

"He's straightening out."

"Good, 'cause he sure as hell has messed up his life."

"Not all of us are blessed with the Midas touch," Matt reminded him. "And, as far as I can see, you're not in much of a position to start slinging arrows." Matt glanced through the glass to Nicole. "Somethin' about the lady doctor that's got you riled?"

Thorne didn't respond.

"Thought so." Matt's smile was positively irritating. "Well, good luck. She doesn't much look like a filly that's easy to tame."

"This has nothing to do with her."

"Right. I forgot. You never get too involved with a woman, now, do ya?" Matt gave an exaggerated wink, pointed his finger at Thorne's chest, then sauntered down the hall after Slade.

Irritated as hell Thorne waited, watching Nicole and Dr. Arnold through the glass, hating the feeling that he was powerless, that the baby's life was out of his control, and that his brother had seen through his facade of indifference when it came to Nicole Sanders Stevenson. The truth of the matter was that she'd already gotten under his skin. He'd kissed her last night not certain of her marital state, not really giving a damn, then taken a flower to her doorstep like some kind of junior high kid suffering some kind of crush. Afterward he'd called her and manipulated the facts just to get a date with the woman. He'd never acted this way before. Never. Didn't understand it. Yes, she was beautiful and beyond that she was smart. Sassy and clever. But deeper still, he sensed a woman like no other he'd ever met. And he'd lost her once. Given her up all for the sake of making a buck.

He was still mentally kicking himself up one side and down the other when Nicole emerged. Her brow was creased, her eyes shadowed with concern.

"How bad is it?" Thorne asked.

Little lines appeared between her eyebrows and he braced himself for the worst. "It's not good, Thorne, but Dr. Arnold is doing everything he can here. He's also linked by computer to other neonatologists across the country."

Thorne's jaw was clenched so hard it ached. "What can I do?"

"Be patient and wait."

"Not my strong suit."

"I know." The ghost of a smile crossed her lips as they walked down the stairs and outside together. Nicole flipped up her hood and held it tightly around her chin. They dashed through puddles to her SUV while sleet pelted from the sky in icy needles.

"Thanks for calling me and letting me know about J.R.," he said as they reached the rig.

"J.R.? That's the baby's name?"

"He doesn't really have one. But I've been thinking that he should be named after my father since Randi is still in a coma and well…who knows what she'll call him when she wakes up." *If she wakes up. If the baby survives.* "Anyway, I appreciate the call."

"No problem. I said I would." She fumbled in her purse, found her keys and unlocked the door.

"Yeah, but you didn't have to go to the trouble of getting a baby-sitter and driving down here." It had touched him.

"I thought it would be best." She flashed him a small grin. "Believe it or not, Thorne, some of the doctors here, including Dr. Arnold and me, really care about our patients. It's not a matter of clocking in and out on a schedule so much as it is about making sure the patient not only survives but receives the best care possible.''

''I know that.''

''Good.'' She blinked against the drops of water running down her face and a twinkle lighted her gold eyes. ''Okay, so now you owe me one.''

''Name it,'' he said so softly that she barely heard the words, but when she looked into his face and saw an unspoken message in his eyes, her throat caught and she was suddenly touched in the most dangerous part of her heart. She remembered his kiss, just yesterday in this very parking lot, and she couldn't forget all the passion that was coiled behind the press of his lips against hers. And that was just the start of it. She knew that within the past day and a half her life had changed irrevocably, that she and Thorne had rediscovered each other and it scared the devil out of her, so much that she couldn't think about it. Not now. Not ever. ''Careful, McCafferty,'' she said, clearing her throat. ''Giving me carte blanche could be dangerous.''

''I've never been one to steer clear of trouble.''

''I know.'' She sighed, remembering how many of her friends had tried to warn her off Thorne way back when. The McCafferty boys were known as everything from rogues to hellions who always managed to find more than their share of trouble. ''Look, I've got to go—''

He grabbed the crook of her elbow. ''I meant it

when I said thank you, Nicole. And I really am sorry."

"For—?"

"For taking off on you way back when."

Her heart jolted a bit when she realized his thoughts had taken the same wayward path as her own. As the wind ripped the hood from her head, she warned herself not to trust him. "That was a long, long time ago, Thorne. We—well, I was a kid. Didn't really know what I wanted. Let's just forget it."

"Maybe I can't."

"Well, you did a damned fine job of it for a lot of years."

"Not as fine as I'd hoped," he said. "Look, I'd just like to set the record straight."

"Now?" She glanced away from him and felt her pulse skyrocketing as the sleet ran down her neck. "How about another time? When we're both not in danger of freezing?"

His fingers gave up their possessive grip and she yanked open the door. Hoisting herself behind the wheel, she pulled the door shut and plunged her key into the ignition. With a flick of her wrist, she tried to start the engine. It ground, then died. She pumped the gas, all too aware that Thorne hadn't moved. He stood outside the driver's door, his bare head soaked, his long coat dripping, as she tried again. The engine turned over slowly, revved a bit, and then sputtered out.

Three more flicks of her wrist.

Three more grinding attempts until there was no sound at all. "No," she muttered, but knew it was over. The damned rig wasn't going to move unless she got behind it and started pushing. "Great. Just…great." And Thorne was still standing there, like a man without a lick of sense who wouldn't come in out of the freezing rain.

He opened the door. "Need a ride?"

"What I need is a mechanic—one who knows a piston from a tailpipe!" she grumbled, but reached for her purse and slid to the ground. "Failing that, I suppose a ride would be the next best thing." She locked the SUV, abstained from kicking it and turned. He took her hand in his, linking cold, wet fingers through hers as they dashed to his pickup. She told herself not to make any more of this than what it was, just an old friend offering help. But she knew better.

Once inside the cab, she swiped water from her face and directed him through town as the defroster chased away the condensation on the windows. He drove carefully, negotiating streets that were slick with puddles of ice as the radio played softly.

"So tell me about yourself." Headlights from slowly passing cars illuminated the bladed angles of his face and she reminded herself that he really wasn't all that handsome, that he was a corporate lawyer, for God's sake, the kind of man she wanted to avoid.

"What do you want to know?" she asked.

"How you got to be a doctor."

"Medical school."

He arched a brow and she laughed. "Okay, okay, I know what you mean," she admitted, glad to have broken some of the ice that seemed to exist between them. "Guess I wanted to prove myself. My mother always told me to aim high, that I could achieve whatever I wanted and I believed her. She insisted I have

a career where I didn't have to rely on a man.'' And
Nicole knew why. Her own father had taken off when
she was barely two and no one had seen or heard from
him since. No child support. No birthday cards. Not
even a phone call at Christmas. If her mother knew
where he was, she'd never said and her answer to all
of Nicole's questions had never wavered. *"He's gone.
Took off when we needed him most. Well, we don't
need him now and never will. Trust me, Nicole, we
don't want to know what happened to him. It really
doesn't matter one way or another if he's dead or
alive."* At that point in the speech she'd usually bend
on a knee to look her young daughter straight in the
eye. Strong maternal fingers had held firm to Nicole's
small shoulders. "You can do anything you want,
honey. You don't need a deadbeat of a father to prove
that. You don't need a husband. No—you'll do it all
on your own, I know you will and you can do and
be anything, *any*one you want. The sky's the limit.''

In the last few years Nicole had wondered secretly
if her need to succeed, her driving ambition, her quest
to make her mark was some inner need to prove to
herself that she could make it on her own and that
the reason her father left had nothing to do with her.

Of course at seventeen, after meeting Thorne
McCafferty, she'd fallen head over heels in love and
been ready to chuck all her plans—her dreams and
her mother's hopes—for one man...a man who hadn't
cared enough for her to explain what had gone wrong.

Until now.

She sensed it coming. Like the clouds gathering
before a storm, the warning signs that Thorne hadn't

given up his need to explain himself were evident in the set of his jaw and thin line of his mouth.

He waited until the second light, then slowed the truck and turned down the radio. "I said I wanted to explain what happened."

"And I said I thought it could wait."

"It's been nearly twenty years, Nikki."

She closed her eyes and her heart fluttered stupidly at the nickname she'd carried with her through high school, the only name he'd called her. "So why rush things?" *Don't be taken in, Nicole. He used you once and obviously he thinks he can do it again.*

He let her sarcasm slide by. "I was wrong."

"About?" she said in a voice so low, she thought he might not have heard her.

"Everything. You. Me. What's important in life. I thought I had to go out and prove myself. I thought I couldn't get entangled with anyone or anything—I had to be free. I thought I had to finish law school and make a million dollars. After that I thought I'd better keep at it."

"And now you don't?" She didn't believe him.

"And now I'm not sure," he admitted, his fingers drumming on the steering wheel as the interior of the cab started to fog.

"Sounds like midlife crisis to me."

He shifted down and took a corner a little too fast. "Easy answer."

"Usually right on."

"You really believe that?"

She leaned back in the seat and stared out the window to the neon lights of the old theater, and wondered why she was in this discussion. "Let's just say I've experienced it firsthand."

"Oh."

"And I swore to myself that the next midlife crisis I was going to suffer through was going to be my own."

He parked at the curb in front of her little bungalow and she reached for the door handle. "I suppose I could ask you in for some coffee, or cocoa or tea or something."

"You could."

She hesitated, one hand on the door handle. "Then again, maybe it wouldn't be such a good idea."

"And why's that?"

She tilted up her chin a bit. "Because this is getting a little too personal, I think."

"And you'd rather keep it professional."

"It would be best for everyone. Randi—the baby—"

To her surprise one side of his mouth lifted in a sexy, damnably arrogant slash of white. "Is that the reason, Doctor, or is it that you're scared of me?"

No, Thorne, I'm not scared of you. I'm scared of me. "Don't flatter yourself."

"Why should I stop now?" He reached for her, dragged her close and started to kiss her, only to stop short, his mouth the barest of whispers from hers. His breath fanned her face. "Good night, Nikki." Then he released her. She opened the door and nearly fell out of the truck. Embarrassment washed up her cheeks as she strode to the door and felt him watching her, waiting until she made it inside. Then he threw his truck into gear and took off, disappearing through the veil of silvery sleet.

Chapter Six

"**D**amn!" Thorne slammed down the receiver and stared out the window to a winter-crisp day where evidence of last night's storm still glistened on the grass and hung from the eaves in shimmering icicles. A headache pounded behind his eyes. He'd been on the phone all morning, guzzling cups of coffee as bitter as a spinster's heart.

He'd bedded down in his old room, the one that had abutted his folks' suite and his brothers had, by instinct, claimed the bedrooms where they'd been raised. But when he'd awoken this morning he'd been alone in the house.

During the intervening hours, he'd called the hospital, hoping for a report of improvement in Randi and the baby's condition. As far as he could tell, nothing had changed. His sister was still comatose and the baby, though stable, was still in danger. He'd hooked up his laptop computer to the antiquated phone lines and looked up everything he could on little J.R.'s condition. From what he could determine, everything that could be done to counteract the meningitis was being done at St. James. He'd even managed to call the office, check in with Eloise and tell her that he hoped a portable office would be set up here, in his father's den, by the end of the day. He wondered what John Randall would've done in a similar situation and, thinking about his father, removed the gift he'd been given from his pocket. The ring winked in the sunlight and Thorne folded his hand over the silver-and-gold band.

"I want you to marry. Give me grandchildren." John Randall's request seemed to bounce off the walls of this old pine-paneled room that still smelled faintly of the elder McCafferty's cigars and Nicole's image came to mind, the only woman he'd ever dated that he'd considered as a mother for his children. And that thought had scared him nearly twenty years ago. It still did because nothing had changed. Oh, there had been a lot of women since he'd dated her; Thorne hadn't been celibate by any means, but no one woman had come close to touching his heart.

Until he'd seen Nicole again.

Not that he wanted a wife or mother for his children or—

What was he thinking? Wife? Children? Not him. Not now. Probably not ever…and yet…the reason he was thinking this way was probably because of his father's dying request, his father's wedding ring, and the fact that his own mortality wouldn't go on forever. Randi's situation was proof enough of that.

Oh, for the love of God. Enough with these morbid thoughts. He looked around this room again and wondered how many deals had been concocted here in the past. How many family or business decisions dreamed up while John Randall had puffed on a black market Havana cigar, rested the worn heels of his boots on the scarred maple desk and leaned back in a leather chair that had been worn smooth by years of use?

This damned metal band had been his father's wedding ring, a gift from Larissa, Thorne's mother, on their wedding day. John Randall had worn it proudly until Larissa had found out about Penelope, the younger woman whom her philandering husband had been seeing. The woman who had broken up a marriage that had already been foundering. The woman who had eventually given John Randall his only daughter.

And now Thorne's mother, too, was dead, a heart attack just two years ago taking her life.

Thorne slid the ring into his pocket and reached for the phone again. He dialed Nicole's number and hung up when her answering machine picked up. Drumming his fingers on the desktop he wondered if she'd managed to get her car towed, if she'd found another means of transportation and how, as a single mother of four-year-old twins she was getting along. "Not that it's any of your business," he reminded himself, bothered nonetheless. He wondered about her marital state—about the man who had been her husband, then forced himself to concentrate on the problems at hand—there were certainly enough without borrowing more. Nicole was a professional, a mother, and a levelheaded woman. She'd be fine. She had to be.

He heard the sound of the front door opening and the heavy tread of boots. "Anyone here?" Slade yelled, his uneven footsteps becoming louder.

"In the den."

Slade appeared in the doorway. He was wearing beat-up jeans, a flannel shirt and a day's worth of whiskers he hadn't bothered to shave. A denim jacket with frayed cuffs was his only protection against the weather. He held a paper coffee cup in one hand. "Good mornin'."

"Not yet, it isn't."

Slade's countenance turned grim. "Don't tell me there's more bad news. I called the hospital a couple of hours ago. They said there was no change."

"There isn't. Randi's still in critical condition and the baby's holding his own." Thorne rounded the desk and snapped off his laptop, turning off his link to the outside world—news, weather and stock reports. "I was talking about everything else."

"Such as?"

"To begin with, your friend Striker hasn't returned any of my calls, Randi's editor at the *Clarion* is always 'out' or 'in a meeting'. I think he's avoiding me. I've talked to the sheriff's department, but so far there's nothing new. A detective is supposed to call me back. The good news is that the equipment I ordered for this office is due to arrive today, and the phone company's gonna come in and install a couple of lines. I've talked to an agency specializing in nannies as we'll need one when J.R. gets home—"

"J.R.?" Slade repeated.

"I call the baby that."

"After Dad?" Slade asked, obviously perplexed.

"And Randi."

Slade gave out a long, low whistle. "You have been busy, haven't you?"

Thorne elevated an eyebrow and remembered that this was his youngest brother, the playboy, a man who had never settled down to any kind of responsibility.

"All I've had time for this morning is a call into Striker and a couple of cups of weak coffee down at the Pub'n'Grub. I ran into Larry Todd down there."

"Why does his name sound familiar?"

"Because he was the man who ran this place when Dad became ill."

Thorne settled into his father's chair and leaned back until it squeaked in protest.

"Get this. Randi kept Larry on when she inherited the bulk of this place."

Thorne remembered, though he hadn't paid much attention at the time. He'd been in negotiations for the Canterbury Farms subdivision at the time and had been dealing with land use laws, an environmental group, the city council and an accounting nightmare because one of his bookkeepers had been caught embezzling off the previous project. On top of all that, John Randall had died and Thorne, though he'd known his father was dying, had been stricken by the news and assuaged by grief. He hadn't cared much about the sixth of the ranch he'd inherited and had left Randi, who owned half of the acres and the old ranch house, to run the place as she saw fit.

"But just last week, Randi called Larry up, told

him she didn't need him any longer and that she'd pay him a couple of months severance pay.''

Thorne's head snapped up. ''Why?''

''Beats me. Larry was really ticked off.''

''When did this happen?''

''A day before the accident.''

''Did she hire anyone else?''

''Don't know. I just found out about it.''

''Someone would have to come and look after the stock.''

''You'd think.'' He saw movement outside the window and watched Matt hiking the collar of his jacket more closely around his neck as he made his way to the back door. Slade frowned. ''Guess I'd better help out with the cattle. I told Larry we'd hire him back, but he's pretty mad. I thought Matt might talk to him.''

''Let's see.''

They convened in the kitchen where Matt had set his hat on the table and had flung his jacket over the back of a ladder-back chair. He was in the process of pouring himself a cup of coffee. ''There's nothing to eat around here,'' he grumbled as he searched in the refrigerator, then the cupboard. He dragged out an old jar of instant creamer and poured in a healthy dose as Slade and Thorne filled him in on everything they'd already discussed.

''We need Larry Todd back on the payroll,'' Thorne said to Matt. ''Slade ran into him today and thought you might talk to him.''

Matt studied the contents of his cup and nodded slowly. ''I can try. But he called me after Randi let him go, and to say he was a little ticked off is an understatement.''

"See what he wants," Thorne suggested.

"I'll give it a shot."

"Convince him."

"I'll try." Matt slowly stirred his coffee. "But Larry's been known to be stubborn."

"We'll deal with that. I've got a call into Juanita to see if she'll come on board again," Thorne said.

"She might be working for someone else by now. Randi let her go after Dad died." Matt hoisted himself onto the counter and his feet swung free.

"Then we'll have to make it attractive enough that she'll come back."

"Might not be that easy," Slade said, sipping coffee from his paper cup. "Some people feel obligated to stay with their employer."

"Everyone can be bought."

Slade and Matt exchanged glances.

Thorne didn't waver. "Everyone has a price."

"Including you?" Matt asked.

Thorne's jaw hardened. "Yep."

Slade snorted in contempt. "Hell, you're a cynic."

"Aren't we all?" Thorne said, undeterred. "And we'll need a nurse. When Randi and the baby get here, we'll need professional help." He was running through a mental checklist. "I'll call a law firm I used to deal with."

"A law firm?" Slade shook his head. "Why in the world would we need lawyers?"

"For when we find the boy's father—he might want custody."

"He should probably get it, at least partial," Matt allowed.

"Maybe, maybe not. We don't know a thing about this guy."

Slade rolled his eyes and tossed the remains of his coffee into the sink. "For the love of Mike, Thorne, don't you trust anyone?"

"Nope."

"If Randi chose this guy, he might be all right," Matt conceded.

"So then where is he? Assuming he knows that she was pregnant, why the hell hasn't he appeared?" The same old questions that had been plaguing Thorne ever since learning of his sister's accident gnawed at him. "If he's such a peach of a guy, why isn't he with her?"

"Maybe she doesn't want him." Slade lifted a shoulder. "It happens."

"Any way around it, we'll need to see about our rights, the baby's rights, Randi's rights and—"

"And the father's rights." Matt pointed out before taking a long swallow of coffee. "Okay, I've got to run into town and go to the feed store. While I'm there I'll pick up some supplies and hit the grocery store for a few things. When I get back, I'll call Larry."

Slade reached into his pocket for a pack of cigarettes. "I'll ride into town with you," he said to Matt. "I want to talk to the sheriff's department, find out what they know about Randi's accident."

"Good idea," Thorne agreed. "I've called but haven't heard back."

"Figures. Look, I've left a message with Striker,

but I'll phone him again," Slade promised, shaking out a cigarette and jabbing the filter tip into the corner of his mouth. "What's your game plan?"

"I'm setting up my office in the den, already scheduled equipment delivery and then I'm going to run into town myself. Visit Randi and the baby." He didn't add that he intended to see Nicole again.

"Yeah. I figured we'd stop by the hospital, too," Matt allowed. "If you get any calls from Mike Kavanaugh, tell him I'll call him back."

"Who's Kavanaugh?" Thorne asked.

"My neighbor. He's looking after my spread while I'm here."

Slade crumpled his empty coffee cup and threw it into the trash. "How long will he take care of it?"

Matt shrugged into his jacket and squared his hat on his head. "As long as it takes." He locked gazes with his brothers. "Randi and the baby come first."

Nicole ground the gears of the rental car and swore under her breath. She wheeled into the parking lot of the hospital and told herself to trust that the mechanics looking at the SUV could find the problem, get the part, fix whatever was wrong, and return it to her soon, without it costing an arm and a leg.

She had half an hour before she was actually on duty and planned to use the time to check on Randi McCafferty and the baby before taking over in the ER.

Setting the emergency brake, she switched off the rental, grabbed her briefcase and told herself that her interest in Randi and the baby was just common courtesy and professional concern, that oftentimes she looked in on patients once they'd been moved from the ER. This wasn't about Thorne. No way. The fact that he was related to Randi was incidental.

She argued with herself all the way through the physician's entrance and in the elevator to her office.

"Something wrong?" a nurse she'd known since she'd arrived at St. James asked as she passed the nurse's station in the west wing.

"What?"

"You look worried. Are the twins okay?"

"Yes, I mean Molly has a case of the sniffles, but nothing a little TLC and a couple of Disney movies won't cure. I guess I was just thinking."

"Well, smile a little when you think," the nurse said with a wink.

"I'll try."

She made her way to the Intensive Care Unit where she looked at Randi's chart. "Any change?" she asked.

"Not much," Betty, the ICU nurse said with a shake of perfectly coiffed red curls. "Still comatose. Unresponsive, but hanging in there. How's the baby?"

"Not good," Nicole admitted as she glanced into Betty's concerned gaze. "I'm on my way to check on him now."

Betty's lips folded in on themselves. The gold cross suspended from her neck winked against her skin. "A shame," she said.

"Where there's life, there's hope." Nicole glanced over Randi's chart, then headed down to Neonatal Pediatrics where little J.R., as Thorne called him, was struggling for his life. As she stared at the tiny baby, hooked up to tubes and monitors, her heart ached. She remembered the birth of her own twins, the elation of seeing each little girl for the first time, the feeling of relief that they were both so perfect and healthy. She'd been jubilant and even Paul, at that time, had seemed happy. He'd looked at her with tears in his eyes and told her, "They're beautiful, Nicole. As beautiful as their mother."

His kind words still haunted her. Were they the last he'd ever spoken to her? Surely not. There had to have been a few more compliments and tender glances before the toll of two high-powered jobs and rambunctious daughters had robbed the marriage of whatever gel had bound it together. Naively Nicole had believed that children would bring Paul and her closer together—of course she'd been wrong. Bitterly so.

"Has Dr. Arnold been in today?" she asked the nurse on duty.

"Twice."

"Good." *Come on, J.R.,* she thought watching the tiny fingers curl into fists. *Fight. You can do it!*

But the baby looked so frail, so small and his vital signs hadn't improved.

"Has the family been in?"

"All three uncles at one time or another."

Nicole had suspected as much. If anything, the McCafferty brothers seemed determined to see that their sister and her son improved, if only by their sheer, collective will. If only it was that easy. "I'll be back later," she said and walked into the hallway, nearly bumping into Thorne in the process. She glanced up to his worried gray eyes and she felt her heart turn over for him as he so obviously loved this little baby.

"How's he doing?"

"The same," she said, turning to look through the glass at the baby. "I thought you'd already been in."

"Couldn't stay away," he said, then cleared his throat. "I had business in town and thought I'd stop by again." He stared at the tiny baby and for an instant Nicole wondered what it would have been like if she and Thorne had had a child together. If things had turned out differently, would they have become parents? Bittersweet were the thoughts, for certainly if she and Thorne had both stayed in Grand Hope, she wouldn't have become a doctor nor would she have her own precious daughters.

"J.R.'s a fighter," she said, touching the back of Thorne's hand. "Try not to worry."

One side of his mouth lifted in a cynical smile. "That seems to be impossible."

"Anything's possible, Thorne," she said and wondered why she felt compelled to comfort him. He turned his hand around and clasped her fingers in his.

"Do you really believe that?"

"With all my heart." Their gazes locked and she thought she might drop right through the floor. The hospital seemed to recede in a fine mist and she felt as if she and he were alone in the universe. Oh, God, this was so wrong....

Her pager buzzed and she dropped his hand. Digging in her pocket, feeling heat wash up her neck, she found the beeper and read the message. "I've got to run." She looked up at him again. "Have faith, Thorne. J.R. will pull through." Why she'd said something she couldn't possibly know as truth, she didn't understand, but she turned quickly on her heel and hurried to the emergency room where she was due to start her shift.

She was immediately accosted by an admitting nurse. "When it rains it pours. Been quiet here for hours, but now we're swamped. You can start with room three. We've got a seven-year-old girl who fell off her horse. Looks like she might have broken her wrist."

"On my way."

"After that, there's a teenager with a sinus infection, and a toddler with a pea wedged up her nose. An RN tried to help, but the mother wants a doctor to look at it." The nurse rolled her eyes. "New mother. This is her first."

"Reassure her that the nurse can handle the extraction and I'll check it out after I'm done with the others."

"Will do—uh-oh." The nurse frowned as she looked over Nicole's shoulders.

"What?"

"Bad news. It's the press. They've been nosing around here ever since the McCafferty accident, but I thought it would die down by now." From the corner of her eye Nicole saw a van for a local news station roll to a stop just outside the windows of the waiting room. "Someone must've gotten wind that the baby was in distress."

"Great."

The nurse's mouth curved into a pained expression. "It doesn't take much in Grand Hope to cause a stir, does it?"

"Never has," Nicole said. The McCafferty family had always been a subject of interest to the townspeople as John Randall had been a flamboyant, once rich man who had actually run for local politics. His public and private life had been the subject of more than one wagging tongue—and his sons had been wild as teenagers, always getting into trouble; but, as the town had grown and the McCafferty children had become adults and spread like seeds in the wind, they had garnered less interest.

"I'd better go see what's up," the nurse said.

Nicole had more important things to do than worry about the press. She pulled the chart of the girl with the broken wrist from the door, scanned the information and, managing a smile, forced all thoughts of Thorne's family from her mind as she spied a frightened blond girl with a tearstained face sitting on the edge of the examining table. Dirt and grass stains were ground into her bib overalls and her mother, a petite woman with worried eyes behind thick glasses stood as Nicole entered.

"You're Sally," Nicole said to the girl who nodded slowly.

"Yes, yes. And I'm her mother. Leslie Biggs. She was riding her horse and fell off just as they got back to the barn. I was on the porch when I saw it, heard her cry...." The mother's voice, gruff and soft, fell away.

"I fell off a horse when I was about your age," Nicole told her new patient.

"Did you?" The girl sniffed, her eyes rounded, but there was a hint of suspicion in her words, as if she

LISA JACKSON   127

expected the doctor to try to cajole her into a good mood.

"Yeah, but I was lucky, I didn't hurt anything except my pride. I was showing off for a boy, thought I could make my pony jump over a pile of firewood and he balked. Stopped dead short. I kept going. Landed in a cow pie." She sent the mother a quick glance. "I think a basic law of physics was involved."

"Ick." The new patient giggled then cried out as Nicole gingerly touched her swollen arm.

"Yep. I never landed a date with Teddy Crenshaw after that. Nope. In fact, he told the story all over school."

"What a creep."

"I thought so. Talk about embarrassing. Now, let's see what we've got here. Looks like we're going to need some X rays..."

Dead tired Nicole, finished with her shift, rounded the corner to her office and spied Thorne, big as life, leaning one broad shoulder against the frame of her locked door. He was less intimidating in casual slacks and a sweater, a leather coat unzipped and gaping open.

She nearly missed a step and her stupid heart fluttered as she caught the intensity of his silvery gaze. Lord, what was it about the man that always put her on edge? The plain truth of the matter was that the man bothered her. He always had. He reminded her of a runaway train on a downhill track, a locomotive that gathered speed to race headlong toward his destination. "You work here now?" she joked.

"Seems like it."

"Seriously, have you been here the whole time?"

"No." He flashed her the remnant of a smile. "Believe it or not, I do have a life of my own. I came back looking for you."

"For me?" She didn't know whether to be flattered or wary. "So you just waited at my office? How'd you know I'd be showing up here? Sometimes I take off directly from the ER."

"Lucky guess."

She arched an eyebrow as she unlocked her door. "Somehow I don't think you ever rely on luck."

"So I called."

"Mmm." The door opened and she stepped inside. He was right behind her. "I assume you've seen your sister and the baby again."

"Yep."

"Any change?"

"Not that anyone's saying."

"I've got a call in to Dr. Arnold."

"So do I."

Rounding her desk, she slid into her chair and said, "Let me check my messages." Thorne waited, standing in the doorway and she waved him inside as she listened to several quick recordings—one from the mechanic. They'd located a part and would start working on the SUV as soon as it arrived. The second call was from Jenny saying she was taking the twins to the park, two more were from specialists she'd consulted with and finally a quick message from Dr. Arnold, giving her an update. She called him back, got his machine again and left another message.

Hanging up, she shrugged. "Nothing. The baby's

stable. His condition hasn't worsened and Dr. Arnold is guardedly optimistic.'' She noticed Thorne's eyebrows slam together, saw his jaw set in frustration.

"There must be something more you can do."

She bristled slightly. "You know that Dr. Arnold's in contact with other physicians and pediatric units across the country—linked up by computer."

"Maybe it's not enough."

"So what do you suggest?"

"You're the doctor."

"Then trust me. Trust Dr. Arnold."

"I guess I don't have much choice," he admitted, rubbing his jaw and scowling.

"There are always choices, Thorne. Just not good ones. Moving the baby to another hospital would be a big mistake."

"Like I said, no other choices."

Feeling as if he were questioning the integrity of the hospital, she wanted to argue, but she didn't. He was upset, understandably so. A man who was used to being in charge, in control of every facet of his life, reduced to the mere mortal status.

"Have a little faith," she told him.

If only he could. As Thorne gazed into Nicole's amber eyes, he felt only a slight case of well-being. But he told himself not to be seduced into a lull, just because he was starting to care for this woman. He couldn't afford to become complacent, not while his sister was battling for her life and the baby was struggling for his. There had to be something more that he could do. "I'll try," he said and caught a shadow of a smile tug at the corners of her lips.

For a second he thought of the kiss they'd shared

so recently, the intimate linking of their hands this afternoon and how it had felt years ago, to make sweet, sensuous love to her. The turn of his thoughts was insane, here in this sterile office, with the sounds of the hospital vibrating behind him, and yet he couldn't keep his mind from straying to a simpler, more innocent time when he and Nicole had made love in the long hay ready to be cut, while the Montana sun had shone on two naked bodies glistening with sweat, flushed from the heat of recent lovemaking and supple with youth. He'd kissed her then and she, giggling, had struggled to her feet, dashed through the waist-high grass and down a soft slope to the creek where she'd splashed through the shallow water and he, chasing after her, had caught her before she'd scrambled up the opposite bank. He'd kissed her again, the cool water swirling and eddying around her knees and then he'd cradled her body, drawn her down and made love to her in the creek, where the sunlight pierced the branches of aspen and pine to sparkle on the clear surface.

Finches and tanagers had fluttered in branches, singing over the babble of the creek and butterflies and water skippers had joined a few bees hovering near the water, but all Thorne really remembered was the silky feel of Nicole's skin against his, the play of her muscles and the taste of her mouth as she kissed him wildly.

Now, staring at her he felt those same male stirrings that had been forever with him when he was near her. No longer a tanned girl running naked through a country field, she was a woman, a doctor dressed in a lab coat, seated in an office that boasted of the professional woman she'd become.

Surrounded by tomes of medical information, a sleek computer, certificates and degrees decorating the walls, Nicole Stevenson had come a long way since she'd been Nikki Sanders, a smart, pretty high school girl with big dreams and little else. As if she, too, in that split second remembered their reckless, jubilant lovemaking, she cleared her throat. "Well, good, then that's that."

"When are you finished here?"

"Just about done," she admitted, and straightened a few files that were scattered over her desk. A forgotten, half-drunk cup of coffee, stained with peach-colored smudges from her lipstick sat unattended near her computer. On a small bookcase, along with medical books, were several picture frames that showed off photos of her daughters smiling and bright-eyed as they posed for the camera.

"So those are your daughters," he guessed, surveying the snapshots of the sprites.

She nodded, her eyes glowing with parental pride. "Molly and Mindy and yes, I can tell them apart."

He laughed. "But no one else can."

"Just their father," she admitted and seemed suddenly uncomfortable. "Or at least he could at one time. It's been a while since he spent much time with them."

"Why?"

She hesitated, sighed and picked up one of the framed photos. "Lots of reasons. Time. Distance. Space...but I'd say the most important was disinterest. Don't quote me, though, I'm just the ex-wife who carries a grudge.'' She set the picture back on the bookcase, ran her finger over the surface as if checking for dust and straightened. "But I'm sure you didn't come here to hear me complain about my divorce.''

"Actually I stopped by to see if you needed a ride. Your rig's not in the lot.''

"Towed earlier. And thanks.'' She was touched that he'd thought of her, then reminded herself not to trust him. He'd left her once before, destroyed all her silly schoolgirl fantasies. "But I've got a rental.''

"When will the SUV be ready?''

"That's the sixty-four-thousand-dollar question, I'm afraid. Don't know yet.''

"Well, if you need another vehicle we've got more than we need at the ranch and I'd give you a ride anytime.''

His eyes held hers for a split second and the back of her throat went dry. Unspoken messages—all male—filled his gaze.

"Thanks. I'll let you know.''

"Do. And there's one more thing.''

"What?'' she asked, looking up.

"Would you have dinner with me?''

"What?'' To his amusement, she actually looked shocked.

Thorne's lips curved into a satisfied smile. "I just asked you for a date. For Saturday night. This shouldn't come as a big surprise. I think we talked about it a few days ago.'' He folded his arms across his wide chest and smiled. "So, Doctor, what do you say?''

Chapter Seven

"I just don't want the rug pulled out from under me again," Larry Todd said. He was tall, about six-three or six-four, with straight blond hair that fell over piercing green eyes. Somewhere between forty-five and fifty, he stood military straight on the porch, a thick jacket zipped to his neck as a raw wind chased down the valley.

"I'll draw up a contract for a year," Thorne assured him. "By that time Randi should be in charge again. Then you can deal with her."

Frowning slightly, Larry gave a sharp nod. "Okay." He slid a glance at the three brothers who had spent the day showing him around the place that he already knew like the back of his hand. If anything, Larry had pointed out the flaws in the ranch—the stretches of fence that needed to be repaired, the way

the soil was eroding on the north side, why it would
be a good idea to sell off some of the timber on the
lower slopes of the foothills, pointing out that buying
a new bailer wasn't necessary this year, while in-
vesting in a larger tractor was a necessity. He knew
about a neighbor's bull—a prize-winner that could be
traded for one on the ranch to mix up the genes of
the herd. Why Randi had seen fit to let him go was
beyond Thorne.

"So, how is that sister of yours?" Larry asked and,
despite his falling out with Randi, deep grooves of
concern stretched across his brow.

"Still in a coma." Slade kicked at a small dirt clod
with the toe of his boot.

"But she'll pull through."

"The doctors think so," Thorne replied.

"And the baby?"

The men exchanged glances. Thorne said, "We
had a scare. He's still not out of the woods, but he's
doin' better."

"Good. Good." Larry tugged at the hem of his
gloves, fitting the rough leather more tightly around
his fingers as the phone blasted from inside the house.
"Draw up that contract and we'll talk again."

He took the steps toward his pickup as Thorne
heard Juanita shout his name.

"Mister Thorne. Telephone!" she yelled and all
three brothers smiled. It was good to have her back.
They'd grown up with her heartfelt convictions, flashing dark eyes and stern sense of right and wrong.

Thorne stepped inside the house. "Boots off!"
Juanita's voice rang from the vicinity of the kitchen.
She appeared, round-faced, her black hair now shot

with strands of wiry gray, wiping her hands on the edge of her apron. "It's your secretary."

"I'll take it in the den." Thorne snapped up the receiver and listened as his secretary gave him an update on his ongoing projects. The development he was working on with Annette's dad had hit a snag with the planning commission, there was threat of a framer's strike and a real estate agent he worked with was "frantic" to talk to him.

By the time he got off the phone his brothers had settled into the living room. They stood in stocking feet, warming the backs of their legs against the fire. Their jeans were grimy and they smelled of horses and dirt. A silver belt buckle—the one their father had won at a long-forgotten rodeo—held up Matt's Levi's and the watch John Randall had worn for as long as Thorne could remember was strapped to Slade's wrist. So they all carried mementos of the man who had sired them—personal gifts he'd bestowed upon them with strings attached—just like the ring Thorne had gotten. Thorne wondered what promises John Randall had wrung from his younger brothers, but he didn't bother to ask.

"What's this about you having a date?" Slade asked, a crooked grin slashing through the dark stubble surrounding his chin.

Thorne met his brother's curious gaze steadily. "I thought I'd take Nicole out to dinner. That's all."

"Sure." Slade wasn't convinced.

A cat-who-ate-the-canary smile was pasted to Matt's square jaw and he shifted the toothpick he'd been sucking on from one side of his mouth to the other. "She isn't exactly your type, is she?"

"Meaning?"

"Kinda down-to-earth, for you." Matt said, obviously amused. "A woman with as much brains as beauty."

"The settlin' down kind," Slade added.

Thorne refused to be galled by his brothers' needling. Neither one had much room to talk when it came to affairs of the heart. "It's just a date," he said, but sensed that there was more involved. He'd had hundreds of dates in his life, spent hours with lots of women and yet tonight seemed different—a little more serious. Maybe it was because Nicole worked at the hospital where his sister and her son were still recovering, but that wouldn't explain the slight elevation in his pulse at the sight of her, the restless nights when he dreamed of making love to her or the fact that he was breaking one of his own cardinal rules: Never Go Back.

Never in his life had he dated a person with whom he'd once before been involved. He figured there was just no rhyme or reason to it. If a love affair hadn't worked out in the past, why would a second try guarantee success? The old adage, Once Burned, Twice Shy, said it all. And yet here he was, planning a date with a woman who had been his lover long ago. He frowned for a second, remembering that he'd seduced her—taken her virginity and after a few short, hot-summer weeks, left her to her own devices.

It hadn't been that he'd grown tired of her; quite the opposite. The more he'd been with her, the more he'd wanted to be with her and it had scared the daylights out of him. At that point in his life he'd had too much to do, too many ambitions yet to be fulfilled. He didn't have time for a serious relationship or a girl he could have easily thought of as his wife.

The truth of the matter was that his feelings for Nicole had terrorized him. But then, he'd been little more than a boy at the time. Now, things had changed.

"If it's just a date, then why all the secrecy, and why did you ask me to—"

"Just take care of it, okay?" Thorne snapped.

"Okay, okay," Matt said holding his hands up, palms outward. "You got it. Two horses, saddled and waiting."

"What?" Slade clucked his tongue. "Horses? Have you flipped? You're taking out a *doctor*. One who practiced in *San Francisco* before she came here. She's a classy, sophisticated lady."

"But not the kind I regularly date?" Thorne threw back at him.

"Not the kind to jump on a horse in the middle of the winter." Slade shook his head as if his brother had gone stark, raving mad.

"Maybe I'm not taking a doctor out," Thorne said, though he didn't feel the need to explain himself. "Maybe I'm taking out an old friend. Nikki Sanders."

"Who's now a mother, divorced, and an M.D."

"Well, you boys stay put and hold down the fort, would you? I'll handle Nikki."

"Or she'll handle you," Matt predicted. "Now listen, be careful with her, all right? She doesn't seem to be the love-'em-and-leave-'em type."

"And we might need to get hold of you. If there's

any change in Randi or the baby's condition,'' Slade clarified.

"I'll have the cell phone with me."

Slade nodded. "Good. Just in case there's any trouble."

"There won't be!" Matt was insistent.

"Let's hope not," Slade said, unconsciously running a finger over the scar running down his cheek. "We've all had enough of that to last a lifetime."

Thorne couldn't disagree. For the past few years, it seemed as if bad luck had become a part of the family legacy. John Randall had lived life full, made and lost fortunes, enjoyed good health and believed that it was his God-given right to be good-looking, rich and powerful. He'd stepped on those who'd gotten in his way, cast off a good woman for a younger model, sired three sons and a daughter; but when fate had turned on him, shredding his fortune, stripping him of a fickle woman, robbing him of his health, he'd been shocked, flabbergasted that his luck had eluded him and the gods of fortune had seen fit to turn on him and laugh, mock him for his pitiful arrogance, in the end leaving him a shell of the man he'd once been.

His death hadn't ended the downward spiral. Randi had lost her mother less than a year earlier. Slade had suffered his own personal loss and Randi's accident, her coma and the illness of her newborn all seemed to be part of a cruel twist of fate.

But it was about to stop. It had to. Randi and little J.R. would recover. The mystery over the boy's paternity and her accident would be solved. Thorne would settle down, marry, have himself some kids....

He pulled up short as he reached the top of the stairs. How had his thoughts gotten so far out of line. Married? Kids?

"Not in this lifetime," he told himself, but felt the pressure of his father's wedding ring deep in the pocket of his slacks and had the vague suspicion that Dr. Nicole Stevenson might change his mind. The truth of the matter was that it was already happening. Even now, he couldn't wait until he saw her again.

Why had she ever agreed to something as foolish as a date, Nicole wondered as she flung on her favorite black dress, then wrinkled her nose in distaste at her reflection in the full-length mirror. The short silk was far too sophisticated for Grand Hope, and yet Thorne was used to big-city women who attended charity balls and gala events.

Her bed was littered with other outfits, everything from black jeans and casual sweaters to this damned dress. "It's just for a few hours," she chided herself as she felt like a damned schoolgirl getting ready for a date with the most popular guy in school. Gritting her teeth, she settled for gray wool slacks, a fitted navy cowl-necked sweater, sterling hoop earrings and black boots. "The everywhere outfit."

"Hey, Mommy. You beau-ti-ful," Mindy said as she slid into the room in her slipper-footed pajamas and drew up short.

Molly was on her heels, sliding headlong into the bed and sniffing loudly from her cold.

"Thanks," Nicole said. "But you're prejudiced."

"What's that mean?" Molly asked suspiciously.

"That you like me just because I'm your mommy."

"Yeth." Mindy nodded, running in circles around the freestanding mirror and Molly raced ever faster, sliding on the hardwood floor.

"Careful," Nicole said.

"Are they bothering you? Girls, come on into the kitchen," Jenny called. "Let's make some popcorn."

"They're fine," Nicole yelled back.

Molly gave chase to her twin, around and around the mirror. Both girls scampered gaily, laughing and shrieking as Nicole twisted her hair onto her head, applied a few strokes of mascara, a light dusting of eyeshadow and a slash of lipstick, then eyed her reflection again. She was struck by her image. Not because she was drop-dead gorgeous, but because there was a light in her eyes, a bit of anticipation, that startled her. For all intents and purposes, she looked damned close to a woman in love.

"Don't even go there," she told herself as she saw headlights flash through the panes of her bedroom window. *Thorne.* Her stomach did a quick nosedive.

"Go where?" Molly asked.

"You don't want to know."

"Where you going?" Mindy asked.

"Out." Nicole bent down to hug them both, careful not to let Molly's runny nose brush against her sweater.

"Here, let's take care of that," she offered, reaching onto the bureau for a tissue, but Molly shrieked, shook her head violently and scampered off.

"It's okay."

Nicole caught her in the kitchen where Jenny was

popping the corn and the smell of butter and sharp
reports of the kernels popping reminded Nicole of a
rifle range. There was a hard knock on the door and
both twins slipped away and ran into the living room
as fast as their little legs would carry them.

"I get it!" Mindy cried.

"No, me!" Molly shoved her out of the way, her
springy curls flying wildly. Nicole caught up with her
just as Mindy, without looking through the window,
threw the door open. Cold air breezed through the
house. Thorne stood on the stoop and Nicole, strad-
dling a wiggling Molly managed to wipe her nose
amid violent protests and wails.

"Sorry," she said, looking over her shoulder, her
hair falling out of its clasp. "Come on in."

"No! No! Mommy, no!" Molly screamed.

Thorne entered as Nicole straightened, wadded the
used tissue and blew her bangs from her eyes. Molly,
her pride wounded, ran to her room while Mindy,
sucking on a finger, looked up at the tall stranger with
wide, suspicious eyes. "My daughter, Mindy," Nicole said, "and the tornado that just screamed down
the hall is Molly."

"Am *not* a 'nado!" Molly protested.

Thorne couldn't swallow a smile. "And here I
thought you were skinning live cats from the sound
of it."

"I *hate* you, Mommy!" Molly screamed and
slammed her door.

Nicole ignored the outburst and tucked her hair into
place. "I'm so glad you got to see my parenting skills
in action."

The door down the hall opened again. "I mean I

really, *really* hate you!'' Bang! The door slammed shut.

''Excuse me.'' Nicole's smile was forced. ''I have to go deal with my daughter.''

''Me, too.'' Mindy followed after her as Nicole headed down the hallway. She felt Thorne's eyes on her back and wished to God that he would have come at just about any other hour of the day. Why did the girls have to act up now? She tapped softly on the door. Molly's sobs were theatrically loud as Nicole entered and found her four-year-old draped dramatically across one of the twin beds.

Stepping over scattered dolls, clothes and toy cars, Nicole crossed the room. ''Oh, honey, come on, it's not that bad.''

''Is...is...too,'' Molly said, hiccuping through her tears.

Nicole gathered her into her arms, straightened and began rocking slowly, cradling her daughter's head into the crook of her neck, mindless of the damage of tears to her sweater. ''Shh, shh, sweetheart,'' she whispered as Mindy, not wanting to be left out, wrapped her chubby little arms around one of her legs and eyed the doorway where Thorne appeared, his shoulders nearly touching each side. An amused smile played upon his lips and he folded his arms across his chest.

''Who he?'' Molly asked crossly, her little face drawn into a frown.

''A...a friend. Mr. McCafferty.''

''Thorne,'' he corrected and Molly's expression turned sour.

''Like on roses?''

"Just about."

Mindy giggled. "It's funny."

"Is it?" Thorne's eyes glinted a bit and he bent onto one knee. "Let's just say it's been a pain in my backside ever since I can remember. Lots of kids used to make fun of me. Now, what's your name?"

Mindy bit her lower lip.

"She's Mindy," Molly said looking down at her sister in disdain, her tears and trauma temporarily forgotten.

"And you're...?"

"Molly." Wriggling she struggled down to the floor and looked up at the stranger with her knowing, imperious four-year-old gaze.

"Mr. McCaff—er Thorne and I are going out."

"You need any help?" Jenny's voice floated into the room and the top of her head was visible over Thorne's shoulder. He stepped into the room and she appeared, arms outstretched toward the twins.

"Jenny, this is Thorne McCafferty," Nicole said and before she could finish the introductions, the twins raced to Jenny's open arms.

"Popcorn?" Molly asked.

"You want some?"

"Yeth." Mindy nodded frantically.

"Good. Let's go into the kitchen and fix up some bowls." Jenny winked at Nicole, muttered a quick "Nice to meet you," and carried both twins out of the room.

"Welcome to my life," Nicole said, turning her palms upward as if to encompass the entire room. "It's kind of hectic."

He nodded slowly. "Between this and the ER,

you're on the go most of the time." One side of his mouth lifted. "My guess is that you wouldn't have it any other way."

"Well, that's where you're wrong, Mr. Mc-Cafferty. In my ideal world I'm independently wealthy, living on a private tropical island and my nannies watch my children while I lie around a pool in the sun sipping frozen daiquiris and having a hunk of a pool boy named Ramon rub the kinks from my muscles."

He laughed and she giggled.

"You'd die of boredom in two days."

"Probably," she admitted, rolling her eyes. "Crazy as it is, I kinda like my life." She tried to pass him, but he grabbed her wrist and held fast.

"It's not crazy at all."

"No?" Her pulse skyrocketed and she felt the warmth of his fingertips against the soft skin adjacent to her palm.

"It's good." His gaze lingered on hers and for a split second she thought he would kiss her again, right here in the house with the kids only a few feet away. Her knees went weak at the thought. "Not many people appreciate their lives nor do they realize how lucky they are." His gaze slid to her lips and she swallowed hard.

"How about you? Do you know you're a lucky man?"

One dark brow rose insolently and her pulse fluttered crazily. His fingers tightened around her wrist. "At this moment I feel very lucky." His head lowered and his breath caressed her face. "Very lucky indeed." He brushed a kiss across her cheek and she gasped. Then he released her. "I think we'd better go now."

Dear Lord. She nearly sagged against the wall, but rallied. "Just give me a couple of minutes to change—this sweater has had it." She escaped to her room on weak legs, closed the door and drooped against it for a minute. What was wrong with her? He'd just touched her arm, for Pete's sake. He hadn't even kissed her and yet she'd nearly melted, like some idiotic, naive schoolgirl. *Just like the girl you once were when you dated him.*

"Damn it all anyway!" Suddenly angry at herself, she ripped off the sweater, looked down, saw that her slacks hadn't escaped their share of damage as well and sighed. From the depths of her closet she found another sweater—a red V neck and threw it over her head and traded the slacks for a long black denim skirt that buttoned up the front. Muttering under her breath, she undid her hair, swiped a brush through it and though it still crackled with electricity, decided she looked fine—good enough for the likes of Thorne McCafferty. She yanked her favorite black leather jacket from a hook on the back of her door and walked into the kitchen where Thorne, still amused, watched Molly throw pieces of popcorn at her sister while Jenny's attention was distracted.

Mindy shrieked. Jenny responded and Nicole couldn't get out of the house fast enough. She slid into her jacket, cinched the belt tight and planted a kiss on each twin's forehead, then did it again when the girls decided to put up a fuss. As she and Thorne walked onto the porch, the twins were wailing loudly, crying, "Mommy...don't go...Mommy, Mommy, Mommmeee—"

"It's nice to be wanted," Thorne observed, holding open the door of his truck as the wind tore at Nicole's hair.

"Always," she agreed, glancing to the house where two little sad faces were pressed against the windowpanes of the kitchen nook. She waved but neither girl responded other than to appear woefully forlorn. "This will last less than two minutes. As soon as the pickup disappears around the corner, they'll be sweetness and light again."

"You're sure?"

"Positive." She leaned back against the seat and eyed him. "Okay, Mr. McCafferty, so where are we going?"

His smile was a slash of white in the darkness. "You'll see," he said, ramming the truck into reverse and backing down the drive.

"Oh, so now you're being mysterious."

"I'm *always* mysterious."

"In your dreams, McCafferty," she said.

"No, Nikki." He slid a knowing glance in her direction. "In yours."

Chapter Eight

"Are you out of your mind?" she asked, shaking her head as Thorne turned into the lane of the Flying M Ranch. The last place on earth she wanted to be was anywhere near the McCafferty home. Too many old memories haunted the spread, too many long-forgotten feelings threatened to jeopardize her emotional stability.

"I've been accused of just that more often than you'd think."

"I thought we were going to a movie or dinner or..." She let her sentence drift off as she wiped the condensation on the glass and stared through the passenger window to the wintry, star-spangled night.

Frost clung to the blades of grass, reflecting in the beams of the headlights. Dried weeds and brambles clung to the fenceposts and in the fields, illuminated

by a pearly moon, the dark shapes of cattle and horses
moved silently. The ranch house itself loomed in the
distance. Warm patches of light glowed from a few
of the windows and the security lamps gave the out-
buildings an eerie bluish tinge.

Thorne parked near the garage and pocketed the
keys.

"Don't tell me, you're doing the cooking," she
muttered sarcastically.

"Hell, no. Wouldn't want to poison you." He
climbed out of the cab, rounded the front of the truck
and opened the door for her.

"Then what?"

"You'll see."

"Once again the enigmatic soul," she observed,
taking the hand he offered and hopping down to the
gravel that crunched under her boots as they walked,
hand in hand, to the stables. Her heart was drumming
by this time, her sense of anticipation spurred by an
adrenaline rush that she found difficult to ignore.
What the devil did he have in mind?

He threw open the door to the stables and drew
Nicole inside. They weren't alone. There, hitched to
the top rail of their stalls were two horses, bridled,
saddled, liquid eyes watching them approach.
"You're crazy," she whispered.

"You think?"

"Certifiably."

"Come on, Doc. Where's your sense of adventure?
Take your pick. The General here, is docile as a
lamb," Thorne said, indicating the tall chestnut gelding with a crooked blaze. "Or, if you'd prefer, you

can have Mrs. Brown, but I've got to warn you, like most women, she's got a temperamental streak."

"Chauvinist," she said.

"Always." His grin was expansive as she, refusing to back down, deftly untied the reins of Mrs. Brown's bridle. The horse's dark eyes appraised her. "It's been a while since I've been in the saddle," Nicole admitted to the high-strung mare as she patted the animal's soft muzzle, "but I think you and I will get along just fine." Mrs. Brown tossed her dark head and the bridle jangled loudly.

"You're sure?" Thorne was skeptical.

"Positive."

"It's your funeral."

"Then be sure to send flowers."

"I think I already did. Well, at least one flower." Thorne laughed as he tied a thick pack and roll to the back of The General's saddle, then clucked his tongue. They led the horses through a back door that opened to a group of paddocks that led to a field crisp with hoarfrost.

"This is absolutely insane," Nicole thought aloud as she undid a few more buttons of her skirt and swung into the saddle. Mrs. Brown sidestepped and fidgeted while the staid General waited patiently as Thorne mounted.

"Where, exactly, are we going?" she asked, holding tight to the reins so that her horse wouldn't immediately spring to the lead. "And don't tell me 'you'll see.'"

"Take a guess."

"I couldn't," she lied because deep in the very most inner part of her she knew the answer, as cer-

tainly as if he'd said the words. Through a series of
gates they walked, the animals anxious, the moon a
shining platter over the dark hills, the creek running
through the foothills. Nicole's heart thudded and she
bit her lip as, at the final gate, Thorne kneed the gelding and The General broke into a gentle lope. Ever
eager, Mrs. Brown bolted, stretching her shorter legs,
trying desperately to take the bit in her teeth.

"Take it easy, girl. All in due time." Leaning forward Nicole patted her mount's shoulder but as the
words passed her lips she wondered if she was talking
to the horse or giving herself some hard but necessary
advice. What was this all about, this moonlit ride
alone with Thorne?

Wind streamed through her hair. Cold air brushed
her cheeks. Her skirt billowed behind her and exhil-
aration lifted her spirits. Oh, so easily, she could be
swept away in the romance, the pure cheeky thrill of
this night ride. But she wouldn't.

Because of Thorne. The man wasn't trustworthy.
He'd proved it once before and she would be a fool
of the highest order if she were ever to give her heart
to him again.

"Never," she vowed aloud.

"What?" He turned his head and astride the taller
horse, his face thrown into relief, his hair rumpled in
the wind, he appeared more dangerous and dark than
ever. No longer a corporate big shot, but a forceful
man, as wild and unbending as this sweep of harsh
Montana land.

"Nothing. It—it's nothing," she said and, in an
effort to get away from the questions he might hurl

at her, kicked her little mare and gave the animal her head.

Mrs. Brown exploded forward. Her hooves pounded. Her legs stretched and retracted. Faster and faster, flying past the larger horse as if he were plodding.

Nicole laughed out loud and cast all caution to the wind. The moonlit night played with her heart and mind. The wind brought tears to her eyes and tangled her hair. She felt freer and younger than she had in years—a girl in the rush of love. Over the rise she rode with the gelding bearing down on them. She cast one glance over her shoulder and spied Thorne, hunched forward, his eyes drawn like a rifle bead on her, his mouth a line of satisfied determination.

"Oh, God," she whispered, then shouted, "hi-ya!" and slapped Mrs. Brown's shoulder with the reins. The little horse shot forward even faster, the ground whirling by in a rush. Over the flat land, across a rise, onward until the trees surrounding the creek appeared—great, black towers bordering the field and looming ever closer. Nicole drew back on the reins and heard The General snorting and blowing as Thorne, too, pulled his mount to a stop.

Nicole tried to catch her breath.

How long had it been since she'd been here? Seventeen years? Eighteen? But it had been summer then, a time of youth and hot, breathless days, when the touch of Thorne's lips against the nape of her neck was as sensual and welcome as a cool breeze.

Her throat swelled at the thought of their lovemaking, so hot, so uninhibited, so long ago. Why had he brought her here now, in this shadowy night with winter as close at hand as summer had been years before?

He climbed off his horse and stood on the frozen ground looking up at her. "Need help?"

"No...I..." She cleared her throat and gave herself a swift mental shake. For God's sake, she wasn't the tongue-tied teenager she once had been. She was a grown woman, a mother, a doctor for crying out loud! "I'm fine," she said, inwardly cringing at the lie because the truth of the matter was that she wasn't fine at all. In fact she was far from it, but she swung down from the saddle and landed on the hard ground only inches from him and determined not to show one sign that any part of him intimidated her. Dusting her hands, she hoped to appear more collected than she felt. "So...why did you bring me here? Just for old times' sake?"

"Something like that."

"Gee, and I didn't think you were nostalgic."

"Maybe you were wrong about me."

Her throat tightened. "I...I, uh, don't think so." She offered him a smile filled with a bravado she didn't really feel. Her skirt was tugged by a gust of wind that rattled through the leafless trees and shivered the longer blades of grass. "I'm just surprised that you seem to feel a need for a trip down memory lane."

"Don't you want to sometimes?" His voice was low, his eyes silver with the moonlight and her breath was suddenly trapped in the back of her throat.

"No." She shook her head. "As a matter of fact, I think it would be a bad idea."

"Oh?" His arms surrounded her and he drew her

close, his nose touching hers. "Well I think it's a damned fine one." His lips found hers and she gasped, her mouth opening and granting his tongue easy access. She told herself that she was being foolish, that being with him was emotional suicide, that getting involved with a man named McCafferty was sure to break her heart all over again and yet she couldn't stop herself. Emotions old and new enveloped her and desire swept through her veins. As if of their own accord her traitorous arms wound around his neck, her eyes closed and she sank against him.

Oh, Thorne…it's been so long….

His lips were sweet warm pressure, his hands big and strong as they splayed against her back, and the combination of the cold starry night and his hot skin was seductively erotic. A small moan escaped her throat only to be answered by his own husky groan.

Don't do this, Nicole, she told herself to no avail. She sensed the horses wandering off, heard, over the ever increasing drumming of her heart, the soft plop of their hooves and the chink of their bridles as they tried to pluck at the frozen blades of grass. Somewhere in the distance an owl hooted and a gentle breeze rushed through the dry leaves of the aspen trees guarding the creek.

"I've wanted to do this from the first time I saw you again," Thorne admitted, his fingers catching in her hair. He tugged, pulling her face away so that he could stare at her. His features were shadowed, his eyes a silver reflection of the moonlight.

"From the first time you saw me again."

"Yes."

"At the hospital?"

"At the hospital."

"Liar." Her breath fogged in the air.

"Never." He kissed her again and this time she responded without the shackles of the past. She kissed him with the same abandon she had as a young girl. It felt so right to have his strong arms drag her to the ground, so natural to turn her head so that his lips and tongue found that spot in the curve of her neck that caused her entire body to convulse.

Warm, liquid sensations streamed through her. Her blood heated, her heart thudded and he kissed her as if he would never stop.

She felt the knot of her belt loosen, noticed when her jacket opened and his hands reached beneath the hem of her sweater. Her back arched as his skin brushed against hers and as he kissed her he scaled her ribs with warm-tipped fingers.

A dozen reasons to deny him screamed through her mind.

Twice as many silenced her doubts. Why not make love to this man? What would it hurt? It wasn't as if she'd never lain with him before, never felt the seduction of his kiss or the power of his body joining with hers.

His tongue was sweet persuasion as his fingers found the few buttons that were still holding her skirt closed. She gasped as his fingers brushed the bare skin of her thighs. *Stop him Nicole! Are you nuts? You can't make love to him. You can't!* And yet as certain as it was that the sun would rise over the eastern horizon, she knew that she would love him again.

Within minutes both her skirt and sweater were disposed of, dropped in a pool on the ground and Thorne was lying above her, kissing her, touching her, causing the blood in her veins to tingle and dance. When she opened her eyes, she looked into a face she'd once loved, a face etched by the years, a face of bladed angles and hard edges, yet in the depths of his eyes and the set of his mouth she saw regret—the tiniest hint of remorse.

The ice around her heart cracked and she blinked against the sting of sudden unwanted tears. Through their soft sheen she saw the moon above him, a bright, frigid disk surrounded by thousands of twinkling stars and she heard the soft babble of the creek.

"I never said I was sorry." His voice was a hoarse whisper.

"Shh." She placed a finger to his lips. "You don't have to say—ooh."

He drew her finger into the warmth of his mouth.

"Oh, no—"

But she didn't pull away as his hot, wet tongue drew anxious circles on her skin as he sucked.

"Thorne—please—"

She intended to deny him but didn't get that chance.

In a heartbeat he released her finger and kissed her hard. Any thoughts of refusal were suddenly stripped away. Her hands found the zipper of his jacket and the buttons of his wool shirt underneath. Her skin tingled, her blood was on fire.

They kissed and touched. Callused fingers caressed her bare skin and she, too, touched him intimately, kissing him and tugging at his clothes, touching him as his jacket and pants fell away. Her fingers traced the deep ridges of his muscles, thrilling to the hard, tight flesh beneath his skin. She kissed the thatch of springy hair upon his chest and was rewarded with the same heart-stopping sensuality as he traced the fragile bones at the hollow of her throat with his tongue, then lowered himself to her breasts where he caressed one button-hard nipple and suckled at the other.

"You're more beautiful than I remembered," he claimed, his breath cool against her hot flesh.

Don't listen to this, don't believe him.... But already she was lost.

Heat burned through her and her mind spun in delicious circles of lovemaking. Deep in the most private part of her she tingled and became moist. Desire thrummed in her blood and seemed to shimmer in the crisp winter air. His breathing was as heavy as her own, his skilled hands rubbing and touching and creating a maelstrom that caused her to gasp.

"I've dreamed of this," he said, lowering his face and kissing her abdomen.

Deep inside she convulsed. Her fingers shot through his hair. Lower still he slid, his tongue rimming her navel. She bucked upward, then quivered with the want of him and bit her lower lip as he kissed the inside of her thigh. Her eyes were closed but as his fingers found the feminine folds of her womanhood and he touched the most sensitive spot within her, she groaned. His fingers were bold, his breath feather soft and seductive, his tongue quick. She arched again and cried out, her fingers digging into the cold, hard dirt as the first spasm hit. Her eyes flew open and the sky seemed to blur—stars and moon blending in pearlescent shards as sensation after sensation rocked her. She was dragging in each breath, spiraling downward, floating....

His fingers dug into her buttocks. He held her close and assailed her again and again, his tongue working exquisite magic, sending her soaring again and again until she was certain her heart and lungs would burst.

"Thorne..."

He came to her. While she was gasping, barely able to move, the sweat of her body drying in the cold night air, he moved upward, spreading her bare legs with his own, kissing her abdomen, her breasts, her throat.

"Now?" she whispered, her blood stirring again.

"Mmm." He kissed her and she responded, felt the male hardness of him pressed against her mound.

"But—"

"Now. You can do it, Nikki." His mouth cut off any further protest. With one quick thrust he claimed her. "We can do it."

She stared up at him and as their gazes locked, he moved, slowly at first, taking his time as the fires within her stoked all over again. Her skin broke out with perspiration and liquid heat seared her. She heard a roaring in her ears, felt the pressure build again. Her mind spun in endless circles and she caught his rhythm, meeting each of his thrusts, opening to him, clinging to him.

Faster and faster. She closed her eyes, thought she was dreaming, cried out and heard his own answering scream as with one final stroke he fell against her, flattening her breasts, his face buried in the crook of her neck. "Oh, Nikki. Sweet, sweet Nikki."

The old ache in her heart reopened at the sound of

his breathless voice. She held tight to him, feeling afterglow seep through her bones.

Finally her heart slowed and she could breathe again.

She'd never felt like this—never with Paul, only with Thorne.

"Well, well, well," he whispered. "That was—" he looked down at her "—worth the wait."

"Oh, was it?" She cocked an insolent eyebrow and imagined that her eyes glowed with a wicked light. "Was it good for you—"

"Don't!" He shook his head and laughed, the deep timbre of his voice ringing in the hills. "Just don't, okay?"

"Just checking."

"Or being a wise guy." He kissed her on the lips then and rubbed her arms. "Cold?"

"Not yet."

"You will be, but I've got something for that." Without bothering with his clothes, he rolled off her, climbed to his feet and whistled to the horses. The General's head shot up and he came close enough that Thorne loosened the saddlebag. From its depths he withdrew a thermos, a bottle and an insulated pack.

"I'm afraid to ask what you're doing." Shivering a bit, Nicole slipped into her sweater and skirt.

"You're getting dressed?"

"If you haven't noticed, it's subfreezing out here." She glanced at the creek where ice glinted between the exposed roots of the trees at the water's edge.

"You're tough. You can take it."

"You be the macho one, okay?"

"Always." She tried not to stare at his nakedness,

refused to notice the play of his shoulder muscles, or the expanse of his chest or the dark juncture of his legs. Instead she concentrated on his actions which included spreading a small tablecloth, handing her a foil-wrapped package and opening the thermos.

"What is this?"

"Juanita's speciality. Soft tacos and Spanish coffees."

"What? Are you crazy?"

"You keep bringing up my sanity, but believe me, I'm as sane as you are. Eat." He sat on the bare ground and she shifted her eyes away from his long, muscular thighs to accept a speckled enamel cup with steaming coffee laced with alcohol.

"I don't believe this." She unwrapped her soft taco and took a bite. A delicious blend of flavors exploded in her mouth. She sipped from her cup and felt the hot liquid slide down her throat. "Tell me this isn't how you treat all the women in your life."

"Nope. Only one." He stared at her for a long minute and she, avoiding looking into his eyes, buried her nose in her cup and drank a long sip.

"So I guess I'm special?" she teased.

"Very." He was still looking at her.

Another long swallow and bite. She wanted to believe him with all the naivete of her lost youth, but didn't dare. "So special it took eighteen years and a tragedy to force you to face me again?"

He was about to take a drink, but stopped short, his cup halfway to his lips. Somewhere nearby one of the horses snorted. "Maybe I didn't make myself clear earlier," he said. "I started to apologize for the past, but you stopped me."

"I know, you don't have to—"

"Sure I do, Nikki. I've got a lot of excuses, but that's all they are and not very good ones at that. This is the here and now. I would hope that you would take me at face value."

"Well that's damned hard to do when you're sitting there naked as a jaybird and I'm having one devil of a time concentrating on your face, if you know what I mean."

"I know exactly," he said, setting his cup aside. Her heart stopped for she knew what was coming. In a split second, he'd grabbed her again, kissed her as if he never intended to stop and, stripping her of her clothes, made love to her all over again.

Nikki, the romantic young girl who still resided deep in the most hidden parts of her, was in heaven at the thought of a love affair with Thorne Mc-Cafferty.

But Nicole, the grown woman, knew she'd just crossed a threshold into certain emotional hell.

Chapter Nine

"Barring any unforeseen complications, the baby's going to pull through." Dr. Arnold's voice was a balm but Thorne, in his relief, wanted to jump right through the ceiling of the den where he'd taken the call. For hours he'd been trying to concentrate on alterations to a contract he'd been faxed by Eloise, or playing phone tag with his real estate agent and tax attorney, but all the while he'd been worried about his sister and the baby.

Then there was Nicole. Always at the edges of his mind. It had been two days since their first night together by the creek and he'd had to rein himself in rather than chase her down, but he had too much to think about to rush headlong into a passionate love affair.

"...so as long as he continues to improve, I would

guess that he can come home in about three days. Since your sister isn't ready to be moved yet, I assume that you've made arrangements for his care.''

''Absolutely,'' Thorne said, though the truth of the matter was that he hadn't made much headway in finding a suitable nanny and the upstairs room that he planned to become the nursery was a long way from being ready for a newborn.

''Well, if you have any questions, give me a call. I'll be checking in on the baby every few hours, just to make sure that he's turned the corner and the nursing staff will notify me of any change.''

''Thanks,'' Thorne said and felt as if a weight as heavy as any he'd ever felt in his life had been lifted from his shoulders. ''Thank God,'' he whispered and leaned his head on the desk. He couldn't imagine what would have happened if little J.R. hadn't survived; he'd never allowed his thoughts to wander down that dark and painful path.

Maybe things were finally turning around. He shoved his paperwork aside and walked in stocking feet out of the den. In the past week he'd changed his habits, giving up the strict regimen he'd adhered to in Denver and loosening up. Randi's condition and the baby's tenuous hold on life had turned his thoughts away from corporate takeovers, mergers, land deals and developments. He'd had less interest in oil leases and start-up software companies than he'd had on this ranch—the land he'd once disdained.

What about Nicole? Isn't she one of the reasons you've found life here idyllic?

Rubbing his jaw, he realized that he hadn't shaved this morning and that it didn't bother him. As he walked down the hall to the kitchen he wondered if he was getting soft or getting smart.

"I tell you I don't want any strangers in this house!" Juanita's voice was firm.

"Thorne's interviewing nannies…they're all referred by an agency I think."

"One that only wants to make money. And what does he know about taking care of babies?"

"Good point."

"My ears are burning," Thorne said as he strode into the kitchen and caught Slade's eye.

Juanita was elbow deep in flour, throwing her weight into a rolling pin that was stretching a disk of dough. Every once in a while she stopped to sprinkle the dough with cornmeal or flour and her expression was thunderous. "That baby, he needs his mother and Señorita Randi—she would not want someone she does not know or trust taking care of her son!" Juanita took off a few seconds and made the sign of the cross. "I have told you this before."

"I haven't hired anyone yet."

"Good." Juanita rattled off a stream of rapid-fire Spanish that Thorne was grateful he didn't understand.

Slade chuckled and shook his head. He reached into the pocket of his shirt and withdrew a folded piece of paper. "Larry Todd's signed on," he said. "I'm goin' to meet him in about—" he checked his watch "—half an hour."

"Good."

"Later this afternoon Kurt Striker is gonna pay us a visit. Will you be around?"

Thorne's head snapped up. "You bet I will. Has he found out anything else?"

"Nothing that I know of, but we'll see." Slade wandered to the back door where his boots were waiting. Nearby Harold, their father's half-crippled dog, lay on a rag rug. Harold thumped his tail and Slade rewarded him by scratching him behind the ears while Juanita slid a warning glance toward dog and man.

"I just washed the floors."

"I know, I know."

Harold, suitably abashed, rested his head between his paws and stared up at her with sorrowful eyes.

"Stay." Juanita pointed at the dog with her rolling pin.

"He's not moving," Slade said.

"Good news," Thorne said and caught Juanita and Slade's attention.

"Señorita Randi?"

"The baby. He's pulling out of it."

Slade let up a whoop and Juanita prayed and crossed herself, her dark eyes filling with tears of relief. "I knew it," she said.

"Does Matt know?" Slade asked unable to stop grinning, his eyes rimmed in red.

"Don't think so. I just got the call. Why don't you tell him?"

"Damned straight, I will."

"Good." Thorne ran a hand over his chin. "I'll run into town—got to talk to some local attorneys about Randi, then I'm gonna stop by the hospital. I'll meet you and Striker back here later," Thorne said.

"Fair enough." With a nod and a crisp salute to

Juanita, the "warden" as he sometimes called her, Slade disappeared through the back door.

"Thank goodness for the baby," Juanita said as she turned back to her dough. "As for that one." She hitched her head toward the door that was closing behind Slade. "He is too...*irrespetuoso*...too—" she waved one hand frantically in the air, sending a cloud of flour around her head.

"Too irreverent."

"*Sí. Irrespetuoso* for his own good."

"You're the one who once referred to Randi's mother as a witch."

"That was years ago and is irreverent—"

"Irrelevant."

"It is fact."

"If you say so."

"I do."

"He's had his own demons to deal with."

"*Sí.*" Her lips pursed and she plunged her hands into the bowl of cornmeal and went about her task, though both she and Thorne considered his youngest brother and the personal pain that Slade had endured.

His thoughts dark, Thorne slipped back to the office, called Eloise and checked in. Her voice was professional and bright, but Thorne didn't miss the stress of the office.

"Buzz Branson's been calling twice a day," Eloise informed him. "Your accountant would like to go over the projected profit and loss on the Hillside View development and Annette Williams left her number twice." His conscience twinged at the mention of Annette's name, though he thought they'd reached an understanding the last time they'd spoken. Obviously not.

"If anyone calls back, give him—or her—the number here," Thorne said. "If I'm not in they can leave a message on the answering machine."

"Will do. Now you probably want to know that there's still talk of a strike by the local carpenters' union. It could involve one of the framing crews, and one of the partners in Tech-Link is under investigation by the IRS."

Thorne let out a long whistle. "You're just full of good news, aren't you?"

"Wouldn't want you to feel unloved," Eloise said wryly.

"Don't worry. As I said, give them the new number—it's connected to two lines and an answering machine, so I'll get any messages. You've got it."

"Will do," she promised and he hung up feeling more dispassionate about his business than he had in years. He looked out the window to the gleaming acres of raw land where he'd grown up. Hooking his thumbs into the belt loops of his jeans, he leaned a shoulder against the window frame and watched a herd of cattle lumber across the winter-dry acres. Shaggy red, black and mottled gray coats moved slowly and every once in a while a lonesome calf bawled.

Thorne had loved it here as a kid, turned his back on it disdainfully when he'd approached adulthood and spent the next twenty years avoiding the place. Now, it got to him. Just as a certain lady doctor did. *You're losing it, McCafferty,* he thought without a trace of despair. *Whatever that edge was that sepa-*

*rated you from your brothers and your old man, it's
getting dull with age.*

And he couldn't let that happen.

Rather than dwell on his changing attitude, he
strode to the stairs and climbed upward to his room.
Some of his clothes had arrived and he thought he'd
best shake himself out of this maudlin nostalgia that
had gripped him ever since seeing Nicole again. He
unpacked his favorite gray suit, starched white shirt
and burgundy tie, then he headed to the bathroom to
shower and shave.

"She hasn't responded yet?" Nicole asked the RN
on duty in ICU. Randi McCafferty lay still, unmoving, her monitors in place, the bandages removed
from her face. She was healing slowly, at least exter-
nally, but she looked worse than ever. Her skin was
discolored and scabbed over, her cheeks still swollen.

"No. We even talked to her and one of the brothers—the one with the dark eyes—"

"Matt."

"Yes, he stopped by earlier and talked to her for
fifteen minutes, but there wasn't the slightest bit of
response." She held Nicole's gaze. "Sometimes it
takes a while. Dr. Nimmo isn't concerned yet and he's
the best neurosurgeon around."

That much was true, and the other doctors who
were attending to Randi, Dr. Oliverio, an orthopedist
and an OB-GYN were outstanding as well. "I know,
but I was just hoping. Since the baby's doing better,
it would be nice…"

Again she looked down at Thorne's sister. *Wake
up, Randi! You've got so much to live for!*

"Unfortunately the press keeps snooping around. Several people from the local paper have called and one woman tried to get in here. She posed as the patient's sister."

"Randi doesn't have a sister," Nicole said, irritated.

"We knew that." The nurse smiled. "Security took care of her."

Nicole wished the reporters would leave Randi and her baby alone. She realized the mystery surrounding Randi's accident and pregnancy was a big deal in this small town, but it seemed blown out of proportion. The patients needed to recover—without the eagle eye of the press scrutinizing them.

"Well, let me know if there's any change." Nicole touched Randi's fingers with her own. "Come on," she encouraged, "you can do this. You've got a little baby who needs you and three brothers who are worried sick."

She made her way down to her office and sighed. It had been a long night in the ER, made more difficult because of her lack of sleep from a few nights before.

After making love by the creek and eating the cold meal, she and Thorne had ridden the ridge at midnight then returned to the ranch. She hadn't gotten home until well after one and then had slept poorly, thinking of Thorne, tossing, turning and pounding her pillow in frustration.

The next day hadn't been any better and last night Molly, complaining of bad dreams and a sore throat had crawled into bed with her. Again, she'd slept poorly and one of the main reasons was Thorne.

She'd remembered kissing him, touching him and making love to him in the cold winter air. Worst of all she thought she might be falling in love with him all over again.

"Foolish, foolish woman," she said, skirting a janitor's cart and rounding a corner of the corridor. She didn't have time to fall in love with any man, much less one who had walked away from her in the past. No, she couldn't fall in love with Thorne. Wouldn't! Gritting her teeth, she forced her mind away from the sexy eldest McCafferty brother and concentrated on the tasks at hand. Her shift in the ER didn't start for nearly two hours, but she had catch-up work to do, patient notes to write on her computer, some calls to make to colleagues, and, as always, she wanted to check on the twins.

At the thought of her girls she smiled though she was concerned as Molly had developed a cough and this morning had been barking up a storm. The trouble with being a doctor was that she knew what complications might develop and she was always worried sick whenever either one of them showed the least sign of illness. "Get a grip," she told herself as she entered her office and shed her lab coat, hanging it over the back of her chair.

To ease her mind she put a quick call in to Jenny and the twins, then switched on her computer and checked her e-mail before writing her patient notes and returning the patient and colleague calls that she retrieved from her voice mail. Her stomach rumbled as she hadn't eaten for hours, but she ignored the hunger pangs and kept working.

Over an hour later she took a break and stopped

by the neonatal care unit where little J.R. blinked up at her under the warm lights. "How'ya doin' little guy?" she whispered as he focused on her. Carefully she picked the baby up and held him to her chest. Tears came to her eyes as she smelled the baby scent of him, felt him snuggle against her, his tiny body swaddled and warm. "You just hang in there, sweetie. Your momma's gonna be so glad to see you when she wakes up."

Softy little coos hung in the air and Nicole thought her heart would break for the poor child whose mother was struggling for life and whose father was nowhere to be found—completely unknown. But J.R. did have his uncles, three rugged men who loved him dearly.

"Got time to feed him?" one of the nurses asked and Nicole couldn't resist. With practiced hands she held baby and bottle and smiled as she watched him suckle hungrily. It felt so right to hold him and she realized how much she wanted another child.

Thorne's child? her wayward mind taunted. *Is that what you want? Isn't he the man you think you're falling in love with? The confirmed bachelor who left you before?*

She blinked hard and fought a powerful wave of emotions as she slowly rocked and cradled little J.R. Was it so wrong to want another baby?

Forget it, you've got the twins; that's enough for a single parent. Would you really want to raise another one without a father?

But Molly and Mindy did have a father, though Paul didn't really seem to give a damn. He rarely called them, never came to visit, wasn't interested in hearing about them. He was remarried now to a professional woman like himself, one who swore she didn't want to be tied down with children. But she was young. Nicole expected she might change her mind.

"There you go," she said softly as the baby quit drinking to stare up at her. "You are precious." She kissed the top of his downy curls and glanced through the plate glass window. Thorne was on the other side, his gaze centered on her, his expression unreadable. Dressed in a business suit, crisp white shirt and perfectly knotted tie, he appeared more unapproachable than he had been, more hard-edged. The terms *shark* and *corporate raider* slid through her mind and she reminded herself he wasn't her kind of man; she'd learned that lesson well.

Nonetheless she felt a flush of scarlet climb up the back of her neck at being caught in such a tender moment. Managing a weak smile she lay the baby back into his crib and hesitated when he began to cry. "Shh. You're all right," she assured the infant.

The nurse stepped forward. "I'll take it from here," she said as Nicole slipped through the door and joined Thorne in the hallway.

"Didn't expect you here," she said, stuffing her hands into the pockets of her white coat.

"Had business in town. Thought I'd check on Randi and the baby."

"He's much better."

Thorne managed a smile. "I see that. I just wish my sister would respond."

"She will. In time."

"I hope." He didn't seem convinced. "Can I buy you lunch?"

She thought about the work in her office. She'd finished most of it and she was hungry. Why not? *Because it would be best if you gave him up right now. He's not in love with you—you're just a convenient distraction while he's in town. But he's going to leave, Nicole. You know it. His life is in Denver.*

"I have to be in the ER in a few minutes."

"So how about a cup of coffee in the cafeteria?" His smile was irresistible.

"Okay. You've twisted my arm," she said with a laugh. Together they walked through the hallways, passing nurses with medication carts, aides helping patients walk and an assortment of visitors looking for loved ones.

The cafeteria was a madhouse, and over Thorne's protests that she should eat something more substantial, she grabbed a carton of vanilla yogurt, a cranberry-pecan muffin and a cup of black coffee while he ordered a turkey sandwich and cup of soup.

Once served, Thorne carried the tray to the end of a Formica-topped table where a few pages of the morning newspaper were scattered. Several nurses were talking at the next table—one of them had obviously just gotten engaged and the others were gushing; clusters of visitors had gathered in several groups and several of her colleagues were debating the addition of another wing and trauma unit.

Nicole slid into a seat near a shedding ficus tree and Thorne sat opposite her. A few of her colleagues cast curious glances in her direction, but for the most part they were left alone. "I was hoping you could help me," he said, unwrapping his sandwich.

"How?" She bit into her muffin.

"As I said before, when J.R.'s released we'll need a nanny."

She swallowed and grinned up at him. "Don't tell me the three McCafferty brothers can't handle one baby."

"We're all busy."

"Mmm." She dipped her spoon into her yogurt.

"I don't think it's gonna be like the movie *Three Men and a Baby* at the Flying M."

"No?" She laughed. "The thought conjures up some interesting scenarios. Thorne McCafferty, CEO, president of the Chamber of Commerce and…diaper changer. Matt McCafferty calf roper, horse brander and…baby burper. Slade McCafferty, daredevil and—"

"Okay, okay, I get the idea." His lips twitched and his gray eyes sparkled.

"Good." She winked at him.

"So you've had your fun," he said around a bite of sandwich.

"It's just nice to be with a man of sooo many talents," she teased.

"Only you would know."

The laughter died from his eyes and Nicole nearly dropped her spoon. Thoughts of making love to him flitted through her mind. Heat climbed up the back of her neck and she swallowed hard at the thought of their recent lovemaking.

"If I recall—"

"Enough, okay? I get it," she whispered, not wanting anyone to overhear the conversation. "Truce."

"Then you'll help me find a nanny."

"I guess I don't have much choice."

"Good. I accept your white flag."

"I didn't surrender, just suggested a truce!"

His eyes glittered with wicked mischief. "Whatever you say."

Still flushed, she managed to change the subject and make small talk through the rest of the meal. Why did she let him get to her? Bait her? Tease her? Flirt outrageously with her? What was it about him that she found downright irritating and incredibly sexual? Good lord, she was becoming one of those foolish, man-crazy women she abhorred! Glancing at her watch, she realized she was running out of time. "Duty calls," she said, standing.

He scraped his chair back. As she discarded the remains of her lunch in the trash bin, he walked with her stride for stride and she was aware how distinctive he looked, a tall man in a long black coat amidst doctors and nurses in white lab coats or green scrubs, or visitors in an array of cotton, denim, rawhide or flannel. There were a few business types as well, salesmen, for the most part, but none were as tall or as arrogantly self-important as was Thorne McCafferty in his crisp white shirt, silk tie, and expensive suit. His presence demanded notice and noticed he got.

At the table where the nurses sat, more than one pair of interested eyes watched him as he held open one of the double doors leading to the hallway, while his other palm rested against the small of her back, as if he needed to guide her through. It was a simple gesture, maybe even a polite, automatic movement on his part, but she stepped away from him as they entered the corridor and was thankful that he dropped his arm to his side. The less personal contact they had, the better.

And yet...

"Has anyone located J.R.'s father?" she asked. "He might have a say in what kind of care the baby gets."

"Not yet." His eyes turned as cold as a blast of winter. "But I'll find him." She didn't doubt it for a moment. Thorne McCafferty was an intimidating force, a man who, if he chose to hunt someone down, would leave no stone unturned in his quest. As she pushed the elevator call button, he touched her shoulder.

She started to step inside, but he took hold of the crook of her arm and pulled her against him. To her surprise he kissed her. Hard. So hard, her knees nearly gave way.

"What was that all about?" she asked, as he finally released her.

"Just something to remember me by."

As if I don't have enough.

Thrusting his hands into the pockets of his coat, he turned and walked toward the front of the building. Nicole, stripped of her breath and dignity in one fell swoop, entered the elevator car. Gratefully, the doors whispered shut and she was alone. *So she wouldn't forget him?*

Well, he needn't worry. Sighing, Nicole leaned against the back wall of the car. Thorne McCafferty was impossible to forget.

Chapter Ten

Kurt Striker looked like the television version of an ex-cop turned private detective—hard features, deep-set eyes that, when they weren't pinning you in his cold, green glare, moved restlessly, his gaze taking in everything.

He shook Thorne's hand in a strong grip that he released quickly. In a jean jacket, matching Levi's, scratched boots and collarless shirt, he stood on the back porch, watching the clouds roll across the western hills. Slade smoked. Kurt didn't seem to mind as he squinted into the distance. Growling deep in his throat, Harold rounded the end of the porch and with a wag of his tail, slowly climbed the steps to settle at Slade's feet.

"Good to finally meet you," Thorne said.

Kurt nodded and Thorne noticed a few flecks of

gray in his otherwise brown hair. "Thought you'd want to know what I've found out."

So there was some information. Good. "Anything." Thorne hitched his head toward the kitchen. "Let's go inside and talk." Slade took last one pull on his cigarette, then flipped it into an empty metal can that rested on a weathered bench. Together they walked into the house where the sharp scent of pine from some kind of cleanser mixed with the aroma of roasting pork.

"Boots off! Muddy boots on the porch," Juanita called from deep in the recesses of the pantry.

"Eyes in the back of her head," Slade grumbled, checking the scuffed leather of his hiking boots. "Forget it."

"Mine're clean," Kurt said.

Juanita was on a new subject as she emerged from the pantry. Carrying two plastic bags of small onions and red potatoes, she kicked the pantry door shut, then dropped both sacks onto the butcher block and shook her head. Pointing an accusing finger at Thorne, she said, "That woman—that Annette. She called again. Insists you phone her, today." With a roll of her expressive eyes, she muttered something in Spanish.

Thorne couldn't hide his irritation. "Next time let the machine answer."

"I did. But I heard it record. I was dusting." Juanita's back was as stiff as an ironing board, her chin elevated a fraction as if she expected Thorne to reprimand her for eavesdropping. "And that is not the worst of it, another reporter called today. Wants to talk to you. *Dios!*" She clucked her tongue, threw up her hands and shook her head as if she couldn't understand the folly of it all.

"I'll talk to them later," Thorne said. Then he turned to Kurt. "Let's go into the living room."

Juanita opened the bag of onions and began peeling them deftly. "Would you like something to eat? A *bocado*? Something to drink?"

"Snacks would be fine. And beer," Thorne said as they walked down the hall. While Slade and Striker made their way to the living room, Thorne shed his jacket, rolled up the sleeves of his shirt and followed.

"So, what've you got?" he asked once they were all in the living room.

Striker stood near the windows. His forehead was creased, his eyes serious. "I don't think your sister was involved in a single-car accident." Thorne's eyes narrowed on the other man. "I suspect another car or truck or some kind of rig was involved."

"Wait a minute. Doesn't this go against everything the police have told us?" Thorne was thunderstruck. He glanced at Slade to back him up.

"That's what I heard." Slade was kneeling at the fireplace, striking a match to the paper and dry kindling.

"It's only a theory at this point," Striker admitted. "But there does seem to be a discrepancy. A few paint scratches on her back fender. No skid marks, no other evidence, but I think it's a distinct possibility another vehicle was involved."

The fire crackled to life and Slade tossed a thick chunk of oak onto the hungry flames. Juanita carried in a tray of three long-necked bottles of beer and a basket of chips. As soon as she disappeared, Striker crossed the room and settled into a corner of the worn leather couch facing the fireplace. Both he and Slade picked up bottles. Thorne didn't. He wasn't interested in anything other than the story the detective was concocting.

"What does the sheriff's department have to say?" he asked, ignoring the fact that his gut was clenching hard, his head pounding. Striker's hypothesis wasn't good news. Not at all. If someone had run Randi off the road or even hit her accidentally, it meant hit-and-run was involved—or worse. It could have been intentional.

"They're not saying much. Though they're still considering all the possibilities. The trouble is, they don't have any eyewitnesses and as Randi's in no condition to tell them what happened, they're not jumping to any conclusions."

"But you seem sure."

Green eyes found his and held. "I said it was just a theory. I'm not sure about anything."

"What about the baby's father?"

"Got a few leads, but haven't talked to the guys yet."

"Who are they?"

"Men she was seen with about a year ago. Seems your sis didn't have a steady boyfriend, at least not recently. She hung out with people she worked with at the paper, and friends she knew from school, but no one she knew realized she was in any serious romance. She never told any of her friends about the guy, whoever he is." He took a long swallow from his beer. "But there are some men who dated her that I'm trying to track down, one's a guy named Joe Paterno, a photojournalist who did some freelance stuff for the *Clarion.* Then there was a lawyer by the name of Brodie Clanton—he's connected to big money in Seattle. His grandfather was a judge at one time. The last guy's a cowboy type she met while helping someone with an interview.''

''His name?''

''Sam Donahue.''

''I knew a Sam Donahue,'' Slade said as he took up a position near the bookcase, leaned his hips against the liquor cupboard and crossed his ankles. ''When I rode the circuit a while. Matt knows him, too, if he's the guy I'm thinking of. Big. Blond. Tough as nails.''

''That's the one.''

''*He* was involved with Randi?'' Thorne couldn't believe his ears.

''Appears so. Haven't quite caught up with him yet.''

Slade scowled and look a long swallow from his bottle. ''Donahue was bad news. In and out of jail, I think.''

''You're right.''

''Hell,'' Thorne snarled.

''The more I learn about little sis, the more I feel like I didn't know her at all.'' Slade shook his head.

''None of us did,'' Thorne said as the front door opened and slammed shut. Matt, bringing in a rush of cold wind, strode into the living room and caught the tail end of the conversation.

''None of us did what?'' he asked, yanking off his gloves and looking from one man to the next. His face was ruddy with the cold and he tossed his hat onto the cushion of a vacant armchair.

Slade introduced him to Kurt Striker and caught him up with the conversation as he grabbed the last bottle of beer and twisted off the cap. "Sam Donahue?" He snorted. "No way. The guy's not Randi's type."

"Oh, so you're the expert now. Tell us, who is Randi's kind of guy?" Thorne demanded, more frustrated than ever.

"I wish I knew," Matt admitted. "Hell."

"What else have you got?" Thorne asked the private detective.

"Not much more, except that your sister wasn't having such a great time at her job, either. Though everyone at the paper's been tight-lipped, some of her co-workers thought she'd gotten into some hot water with the editors."

"How?" Thorne asked, his eyebrows slamming together.

"Good question. I've got copies of all the columns she wrote for the past six months, but those are only the ones that were in print. According to her friend Sarah Peeples who writes movie reviews, Randi had about two weeks' worth of columns that she'd written but hadn't yet been printed. No one has seen them. And there was talk of some kind of project she was working on, though the paper denies it. Again, no one's seen any copies of it."

"Except maybe Randi."

"And she's not talkin'," Matt observed, his mouth a grave line as he leaned against the bookcase and the fire crackled and hissed.

"She writes advice to the heartbroken for God's sake!" Slade interrupted.

"And what else?" Striker thought aloud.

Matt frowned down at his beer. "Now wait a minute. You said that Randi's vehicle *might* have been struck, but no one knows if it was intentional or not. It's a pretty big leap to go from a single-car accident because the driver hit black ice to some kind of…what? Attempted murder?"

"All I'm saying is that there might have been another vehicle involved and if there was, the driver is, at the very least, guilty of hit-and-run. From there it only gets worse."

"*If* she was hit." Matt's gaze fastened on the private investigator. He was obviously skeptical.

"Right."

"I think we're making big assumptions here."

"Just checkin' out all the possibilities," Slade argued. "We owe it to Randi."

"God, I wish she'd wake up." Matt straightened and shoved a hand through his hair in frustration.

"We all do." Thorne looked from one brother to the other. "But until she does, we've got to keep trying to figure this out." To Striker, he said, "Keep at it. Talk to anyone you can. We need to find the father of Randi's baby. If there's any way you can find out the blood type of the men she was involved with, we could at least eliminate some of the possibilities."

"Already doin' it," Striker admitted.

"How do you do that?" Matt said.

Kurt sent him a look silently telling him he didn't want to know.

"Just handle it." Thorne wasn't sure he liked Kurt Striker, but he believed the man would do what had to be done to dig up the truth. That was all that mattered. He didn't even care if the law was bent a little, not if Randi's life was truly endangered by someone with a grudge. But *who?*

Striker nodded. "Will do. And I'm gonna try to find those missing columns. I don't suppose any of you know if she had a laptop computer?"

Slade lifted a shoulder, Matt shook his head and Thorne frowned.

"Nothin's on her desktop."

"How do you know that?" Matt asked.

"I checked."

"You broke into her apartment?" Matt looked from one of his brothers to the next. "Hey—isn't that illegal? Randi'll kill us if she ever finds out."

"Or someone doesn't take care of that first." Striker took a long, final tug on his long-necked bottle.

"Wait a minute...." Matt stared at Thorne incredulously. "Don't you think we're leaping to conclusions, here? I mean she had a wreck, she got hurt, but I don't see that there's any hint of foul play."

"You don't know there isn't."

"But why? Everyone she ever met liked her and as Slade said, she gave advice to the lovelorn for crying out loud. Not exactly cloak and dagger stuff. It's not like she was writing scandal sheets or political exposes."

"It was more than just lovelorn cra—stuff," Slade clarified. "Her column was about single people—"

"Right. I know," Matt snapped.

"But the point of it is that none of us really knew what she was doing with her life, did we?" Thorne pushed up his sleeves. "She didn't even tell us she was pregnant. Now, there's a chance someone either by accident or intent, was involved in her accident. We just have to find out who."

"And *why*." Matt threw up a hand in exasperation. "Don't we need a motive?"

"Not if it was an accident and someone was just scared to come forward." Slade drained his bottle.

Matt's back was up. "Well then, looking into her computer records and breaking into her apartment wouldn't be necessary, would they?"

"Hey! Anything's worth a try!" Slade shot to his feet and walked up to his brother. "Don't you think we should look into everything?" Slade's color was high, his jaw set, just the way it had been when they'd been kids growing up and were about to start throwing punches.

Matt held his ground. Even managed that slow, go-ahead-and-try-it smile that both his brothers found so damned irritating.

"We don't know a lot," Slade said through clenched teeth. "Kurt's gonna help us get to the bottom of it. You got a problem with that?"

A muscle worked in Matt's jaw and his brown eyes narrowed on his younger brother. "No problem. I just want what's best for Randi and J.R., you know that. And some son of a bitch is responsible for her condition. I want him found and nailed. You bet I do. But that's what the sheriff's department is for."

"Unless they're sittin' on their butts," Slade said.

"Right. But I don't think we should go on a witch hunt until we're sure there's a witch."

Kurt stood. "Don't worry. If there is one, I'll find him...or her."

"Good." Slade took a step back.

"That settles it. Do what you have to," Thorne said, then walked Striker to the door where they shook hands again. The phone rang as the door shut behind the investigator. "I'll get it," Thorne said, striding to the den. He had work to do and couldn't let his brothers' tempers deter him.

"Hello?" he nearly shouted.

"Boy are you in a bad mood." Annette's voice sang through the wires.

He felt instantly weary. "Just busy."

"When are you coming back to Denver?" Good old Annette. She didn't beat around the bush.

"Don't know," he admitted, resting one hip on the corner of his father's desk and letting his leg swing free. The thought of returning to his office and the penthouse and the whirl that was his life in the Mile-High City held little appeal right now.

"So you like being a cowboy again?" she asked and laughed without a trace of acrimony—as if nothing had changed between them.

"Believe it or not, I do like it here," he said with complete honesty. "Don't think I'm much of a cowboy."

"Oh, darn and I was just pressing my denim skirt and checked blouse."

"Was there something you wanted?"

"Mmm. Actually there was. Daddy's forgiven you."

Thorne doubted it.

"And he still wants to work with you."

"So, why didn't he call me?"

"Because I wanted to. To make sure there were no hard feelings."

"None on this end." And yet he didn't trust her.

"Good. And don't worry, Daddy will call you himself. Let me know when you're in town. Oh, and Thorne—take off the bolo, it's not your style."

"I'm not wearing a tie of any kind."

"Oh, dear. That's worse yet. Well, so long, pardner," she said with a laugh. There was a click on the other end of the line and he was left holding the receiver and wondering why she'd bothered to call.

"Doesn't matter," he reminded himself because he didn't feel a thing for her; never had. Nor had he experienced any special bond with the women he'd dated in the past few years. Until he'd seen Nicole again. From the moment he'd first laid eyes on her in the hospital, he'd been taken with her. He wondered what she was doing right now, considered dialing the number he'd already committed to memory, then reminded himself that he had other things that had to be done.

For the next two hours he returned phone calls, e-mails and faxes, but his concentration wasn't as focused as it usually was and thoughts of his sister and her baby kept sneaking into his mind.

When he'd finally hung up from a call with his attorney Thorne leaned the desk chair back so far it protested. Drumming his fingers on the curved arm, he stared through the window into the night. A dozen questions burned through his brain. Why was Randi in Montana? Who was the baby's father? Did the accident involve another vehicle? Would Randi and the baby be okay? When would she come out of the coma?

He had no answers to any of those and another thought, one he'd kept steadfastly at bay, burrowed into his brain. He wondered what Nicole was doing tonight. "Forget it," he growled at himself, but his mind kept wandering back to the night they'd made love, their bodies glistening with sweat under the cold winter stars. When could he see her again? He glanced at the phone, mentally cursed and wondered how she'd managed to get under his skin.

He remembered taking her into his arms in the parking lot of the hospital and her small gasp of surprise as he'd kissed her; he remembered the way she'd moaned when he'd made love to her by the creek; and he remembered seeing her hold the baby in the nursery, looking down at the child's tiny face, smiling and whispering to the infant, so naturally as if she were his mother. The effect on Thorne had been immediate and heart stopping.

If he didn't know better, he'd think he was falling in love. But that was ridiculous. He wasn't the kind of man to fall into that kind of trap.

He wasn't ready to tie himself up with one woman, not yet. He had too much to do.

Oh, yeah? And what's that? Make another million or two? Turn a losing company into a winning corporation? Develop another subdivision? Go back to an empty penthouse in a city where your only friends are business associates?

Standing, he raised his arms over his head and

stretched, his spine popping a bit. Of course he'd return to Denver and resume his life. What was the other option? Stay here? Marry Nicole?

He froze. *Marry Nicole?* Dr. Stevenson? Impossible! No way!

And yet the thought held a seductive and dangerous appeal.

"This is ridiculous," Nicole told herself as her shift ended and she opened the door to her office. Thankfully it had been a slow day in the emergency room, with only a broken hip, an asthma attack, a dog bite, a case of severe appendicitis and two kids with contusions and concussions in a bicycle-car mishap. In the lulls between patients she'd been able to catch up on her notes, check on some of the patients she'd admitted earlier including Randi and J.R., and think about Thorne McCafferty.

She'd been thinking about him a lot lately. Too much. She sat in her desk chair and twiddled a pen. They'd talked on the phone a couple of times since they'd made love near the creek and, of course, he'd come for lunch that day and run into her at the hospital time and again when he'd been visiting his sister. He'd always stopped by to see her and consequently a few rumors had already started and some of her coworkers had winked at her whenever he'd appeared.

"Forget him," she told herself, knowing it was impossible. He was getting to her all over again, even though he'd taken off on her once before. He'd given no excuses, just taken off and bailed out to chase after dreams of making his mark in the world, leaving her heartbroken. In spite of this, she was fascinated by the man. Stupidly fascinated, she reminded herself. She couldn't take a chance on letting him hurt her again.

She finished her paperwork, then perused photocopies of a few of Randi McCafferty's columns that Clare Santiago, Randi's OB-GYN, had given her. Out of curiosity about her new patient and the hoopla created by the local press, Clare had found some of the articles on the Internet and printed them out.

Now, as Nicole scanned the columns, she smiled. Randi gave advice freehandedly. With tones of irony and sarcasm, she dished out levelheaded counsel to single people who had written to her concerning their love lives, work problems, past relationships, or troubles juggling hectic schedules. Randi borrowed literary clichés, old adages and peppered the column with hip slang; but most of the advice was given tongue-in-cheek and showed off her clever, if sometimes cutting, wit. Nicole actually laughed at a few of the passages, and wondered if any of Randi's headstrong older brothers had ever been on the receiving end of her razor-sharp tongue.

If only the woman lying in ICU could talk. Tucking the articles into a file, Nicole decided to call it a day. She snapped off her computer and desk lamp, then stretched and walked into the hallway. Before she'd go home, she would look in on Thorne's sister—the silent, comatose woman whose advice had touched millions.

Outside the doors of ICU, Nicole found Slade and Matt McCafferty waiting impatiently.

"Hi." Matt was standing near a post and quickly removed his hat.

Slade, seated in a chair in the small waiting area, quickly tossed aside a battered magazine and climbed to his feet.

"I thought I'd check on your sister before I went home."

"There's no change," Slade grumbled. "I was just in there and the doctors are talking about setting her broken bones now that the swelling's gone down." He looked down at his hands as they worked the brim of his hat. "She looks like hell."

"But improving," Nicole countered. "These things take time."

"Well, I wish she'd wake up." Matt's brow was furrowed with deep lines of worry. He motioned toward the closed doors. "Thorne's with her now."

"He is?" Why did her heart do a stupid little flip at the mention of his name?

"Yep." Slade checked his watch, stared at the face a second and his lips rolled in on themselves. "He should be out soon if you want to talk to him."

One side of Matt's lips curved upward. "So what is the deal with you and Thorne?"

"Is there a deal?" she said, matching his grin.

"I'd say so." Slade gave a quick nod. "Never seen Thorne so...content."

"He's not content," Matt said, shaking his head. "Hell, that guy doesn't know the meaning of the word. But he is less restless. Not as quick to jump down someone's throat. Distracted."

"Is that right—"

The doors flew open and Thorne, in jeans and a leather bomber jacket, burst through. His face was a thundercloud, his jaw set, his eyes narrowed until his gaze landed full force on Nicole.

"Something wrong?" she asked.

"Yeah, there's something wrong." He hitched a thumb toward the doors swinging shut behind him. "She's still in a coma and looks like hell. The doctors keep saying she's doing as well as can be expected, but I don't know if I can believe them. It's been over a week since she was brought in here."

"Everything that can be done is being—"

"Is it?" he demanded and she was aware of how much taller he was than she. "How do I know that?"

"I thought we'd been through this—the competency of the staff, the efficiency of the hospital, the time it takes the body to heal—"

"Enough." He glared down at her, then rammed his hands through his hair in frustration. "Hell!"

"What is it you want?" she demanded.

"You mean other than my sister and her child to be well, the baby's father located, the truth about her accident figured out, and world peace?"

"Is that all?" She lifted an imperious eyebrow and held his arrogant, demanding and ultimately irresistible gaze fast.

"No. I could use a cup of coffee, too!"

"Well, I'll find one for you, just as soon as I heal your sister and finish the last-minute details on the world peace thing," she snapped, hearing a snicker behind her. Turning on her heel, she found Slade trying and failing to swallow a smile. "Something funny?"

"Nothin' at all. In fact I'm enjoyin' the show. Not often someone puts ol' Thorne in his place."

"Is that what she's doing?" Thorne asked, then before Nicole could protest, grabbed her by the crook of the elbow and propelled her down the hallway. "You, two," he called over his shoulder, "can leave. I'll catch up with you later."

"Wait a minute. What do you think you're doing?" she demanded as he forced her around a corner to a tiny alcove with a window seat and two potted plants.

"This." He didn't waste time, just lowered his head and kissed her so hard she couldn't breathe.

Her bones began to melt and she told herself this was insane, that he had no right to manhandle her anywhere, but especially not here, in the hospital where she was working. Yet there was a part of her that responded to his spontaneity, the thrill of a man wanting her enough to drag her into the comparative privacy of the alcove.

His mouth was pure magic—warm, insistent pressure. She kissed him back, her lips parting to accept his tongue, her heart pounding a wild, frantic cadence as her beeper went off.

She jerked back and saw the amusement in his eyes. "Couldn't resist," he said by way of explanation as she reached into her pocket for her pager.

"Maybe you should learn to exercise some control." She checked out the digital display of numbers and recognized Dr. Oliverio's extension.

"Ha." He let out a short laugh. "I don't have a helluva a lot of that around you," he admitted. "Nor, *Doctor,* do you."

"You surprised me, that's all. Look, I have to go."

"Emergency?"

"I don't know," she admitted, "but I'd better check it out."

His grin was pure mischief as he pulled her to him and kissed her soundly again. "I'll call you later."

"Fine." She turned and found two aides walking down the hallway and pretending they hadn't seen anything, but the smiles they tried to disguise and the twinkle in their eyes as they exchanged knowing glances convinced her otherwise.

Clearing her throat she marched down the corridor toward her office and reminded herself, for what seemed the fiftieth time, she wasn't going to get involved with Thorne McCafferty.

But a little voice inside her head had the audacity to insinuate that it was too late. She was already more involved than any sane woman would allow herself to be.

Chapter Eleven

"I'll let you know," Thorne said, raining what he hoped appeared to be a patient smile on the woman seated in his father's favorite recliner. Her name was Peggy, she'd moved to Missoula from Las Vegas this past year and was now in Grand Hope. As far as he could tell her experience with young babies had been limited to raising her own children, who were now grown, and spending a few years as an aide in a day-care center. Her other jobs had included working as a supervisor in a cannery in California and as a maid for a hotel while she'd lived in Nevada. She was pleasant enough, he supposed, but he wasn't convinced she was the woman for the job of living at the ranch and taking care of little J.R. "I'm still interviewing."

She smiled as she stood and tossed her shaggy

graying hair over her shoulders. "Well, let me know. You've got my number."

"It's on the résumé."

She stuck out her hand and he clasped it, noticing that she wore a ring on every finger. Her makeup was thick, her fingernails long and polished a deep maroon. "Thanks." She strolled out of the living room, her slim hips rolling beneath tight jeans. At the door front, he handed her a battered suede coat and a heavy fringed purse. She slung the strap over her shoulder and headed out the door.

Boots pounded on the stairs. "Well?" Matt asked as he appeared from the second story. He looked expectantly at his brother. "Found someone?"

"Not yet." Thorne glanced through the window and watched Peggy climb into a huge station wagon that had enough grime on it that some wise guy had written Wash Me on the back windshield. She paused to light a cigarette and blow out a geyser of smoke before putting the car into gear and gunning the engine. No, Peggy Sentra wouldn't do. Nor would the other two women he'd already met.

"You interviewed three people."

"And I'll probably have to talk to a dozen or so more." The three women he'd seen, Peggy and the two others, had barely made an impression on him other than they were entirely unsuitable to take care of his newborn nephew and were a far cry from what he'd expected. "I've already left a call on the voice mail of the agency."

"Little J.R.'s coming home tomorrow."

"I know, I know," Thorne snapped. "And I guess

the four of us, you, Slade, Juanita and I will just have
to juggle the duties until we find someone.''

"Hey, whoa there,'' Matt said, holding up both
hands palms outward. "I'm gonna be out tomorrow—
got to fix the fence on the north end of the property
before we move the herd. Slade, Adam Zolander and
Larry Todd are supposed to help me. The day after
that I've got to run back to my own spread, so you'd
better count me out until I get back.''

Thorne frowned, but didn't argue. Matt owned a
ranch near the Idaho border, a place he'd barely been
able to afford, and yet he'd scraped together enough
money for a down payment and talked the previous
owner into taking a contract on the rest. Matt was
known to work sixteen or eighteen hour days—all for
that scrap of hilly land and a small run-down farm-
house. Thorne had never understood Matt's connection with the land, his need to ranch his own place,
but there it was. Whereas Thorne had learned at an
early age that acreage was valuable because it held
its worth or could be developed and sold for a profit,
Matt seemed to believe that he was somehow linked
to the soil.

"All right. You're out.''

"And so is Slade tomorrow, so, unless you can con
Juanita into changing diapers and burping the baby,
looks like you're the chosen one, the nanny.'' Chuck-
ling, he grabbed his hat. "And the nursery's just
about ready. I got the crib and changing table and
bureau together, but we still need some staples—for-
mula, diapers, baby powder and sleepers.''

"Already ordered,'' Thorne said.

"Good.''

Laughing to himself, Matt threw on his jacket, then walked outside. Thorne headed back to the den. Time for Plan B.

The phone rang and Nicole, already reaching for her keys, grabbed the receiver instead. "Hello?"

"Hi." Recognizing Thorne's voice she leaned against the window and smiled to herself. Why her lips curved upward, she didn't understand, but she didn't fight it as she stared into the night-darkened backyard. The girls clamored around her and to quiet them she pressed the index finger of her free hand to her lips.

"I need your help."

"*You* need *my* help?" She smothered a smile. There was something amusing about the CEO of McCafferty International asking for any kind of advice or aid.

"Absolutely. J.R.'s being released from the hospital tomorrow and that'll be quite a change around here."

She eyed her two dynamos. "You have no idea."

"I thought maybe you could give me some pointers."

"Oh, sure." She laughed as she watched Molly chase after Mindy with a rubber snake. Mindy shrieked in mock horror. "Don't you know that I do this motherhood thing day by day?"

"Can we discuss it over dinner?"

"I have the girls."

"Bring 'em."

She laughed out loud. "I don't think you understand what you're asking."

"Probably not, but maybe it's time I learned. I could pick you up and—"

"No, we'd better meet. I finally got the SUV back and it's ready to go *and* equipped with safety seats. Besides that I have been known to cut out early if the twins—" she was eyeing the girls as they streaked by with her I'm-the-mom-and-you'd-better-listen-to-me scowl "—make the mistake of acting up, which I'm *sure* won't happen tonight. They wouldn't dare."

Mindy bit her lower lip, but Molly ignored the warning and wriggled the fake-looking snake in her sister's face. "I already told the girls I'd take them to the Burger Corral. It's on the corner of Third and Pine."

"I know where it is," he said dryly. "I grew up here. But I was thinking of something a little quieter."

"Believe me, when you've got four-year-olds, you don't want quiet."

Molly was tugging at the edge of her jacket. "Come *on*, Mommy."

"Look, if you want to meet us, do," she invited. "We're on our way right now."

"I'll be there in half an hour."

Nicole hung up and told herself she wasn't thinking clearly. Hadn't she already told herself not to get involved with Thorne, that just because they'd shared a few kisses and quiet conversations and made love wasn't any reason to put on her old pair of rose-colored glasses again—the ones with the cracked lenses from trusting Thorne McCafferty before? But there was something about the man she found so damned irresistible it was dangerous. More than dangerous—emotional suicide. "Come on kids, put your jackets on."

The phone rang again almost instantly and Nicole picked up thinking that Thorne had changed his mind. "Want to back out?" she teased.

"I think it's a little too late for that now, isn't it?" Paul's voice was a damper on her good mood and she steeled herself for what was certain to be a tense conversation.

"I was expecting someone else to call."

"Then I'll make it short." His voice had all the warmth of a blue norther and Nicole wondered how she'd ever once thought she'd loved the man.

"Okay."

"It's about visitation rights."

"What about them?" she asked, her fingers clenching the receiver in a death grip, the knot in her stomach tightening as it always did when she and Paul began to argue—which was nearly every time they spoke.

"I know that I'm supposed to have the girls every other Christmas and each summer."

"That's right." Her heart began to pound. She couldn't believe it but thought he might actually be angling for custody. Oh, Lord, what would she do if she lost the twins?

"But Carrie and I are going to visit her folks in Boston over the holidays and this summer we've planned a trip to Europe. Her company is sending her to a convention in Madrid and we thought we'd take the opportunity to see France, Portugal and England while we're there. So, there would be four weeks right in the middle of summer where we couldn't take the twins.''

As if parental responsibility were an option.

She glanced at her daughters, now struggling into their jackets and her heart broke when she thought about them growing up without a father.

"You know we'd *love* to have them if it were possible, but Carrie's got to think of her career.''

"Of course she does.''

"Just like you do, Nicole. Like you always have.'' There it was: the inevitable dig. What was deemed noble for Carrie was somehow disgraceful for Nicole because she was a mother. She let the little barb slide. No reason to reduce the conversation to hot words at this point. "Don't worry about it,'' she said, though her throat was thick. "It would probably be best if they stayed with me.''

"Actually, I think so. It would be hard on Molly and Mindy to uproot them and drag them here to the apartment. They're not used to a big city or being confined to a few rooms. With both our jobs it would make it really difficult and—''

"Look, I understand, but I've got to run. Do you, uh, want to speak to the girls?'' She couldn't stand to hear one more minute of his rationalizations for giving up his children. They were his daughters, for God's sake! So precious. So wonderful. And they deserved better.

"Oh.'' A pause. "Sure.''

Without much enthusiasm, she put each of the twins on the phone, let them speak to the stranger who had sired them and within three minutes was back on the phone. "I'm already late and I've really got to run now, but we'll work the visitations out."

"I knew I could count on you." The words echoed through her mind and she toyed with the question of what he would do if he couldn't rely on her.

"I'm glad you understand." Relief was heavy in his voice.

"Goodbye, Paul." She hung up incensed and helped Mindy zip up her jacket. "Come on, kids, let's roll."

"You mad, Mommy?" Mindy asked as Nicole slung the strap of her purse over her shoulder. Catching sight of her reflection in the window, she understood her daughter's concern. Her eyebrows were slammed together, her mouth pursed tight at the corners.

"Not anymore. Come on, let's get into the car." She opened the door and the twins swarmed through, their chubby legs flashing, their shoes pounding on the back porch, their laughter and giggles ringing through the night air.

"I get shotgun!" Molly cried.

"No, me—" Mindy started to pout.

"You're both in the back seat, in your car seats and you know it," Nicole said. "Remember?"

"But Billy Johnson gets to ride in the front seat," Molly said. Billy was a wild-haired boy in their preschool.

"So does Beth Anne."

Another friend.

"Well, you don't." Nicole helped strap them into their respective seats, then climbed behind the wheel. She paused long enough to reapply her lipstick, then

twisted on the ignition and grinned as the SUV roared
to life. As she put the rig into reverse she felt a twinge
of apprehension about meeting Thorne again.
Whether she liked it or not she was in some kind of
relationship with him and that thought worried her.

"It's not a date," she told herself.

"What?" Molly demanded.

"Nothing, sweetie, now you girls figure out what
you want to get for dinner," she said and silently
added, *and I'll try to figure out what to do with
Thorne McCafferty.*

Within fifteen minutes she'd driven to the small
restaurant, parked in the crowded lot, then shepherded
her girls to a corner booth near the soda fountain.
With the efficiency of the mother of twins, Nicole
helped the girls out of their jackets and let them wander to the video games where a group of boys who
looked about eight or nine were trying to best each
other and the sounds of bells, whistles and simulated
gun reports punctuated the buzz of conversation, clat-
ter of flatware and rattle of ice cubes from the self-
serve soda machine.

Somewhere, above it all, there was the hint of music, some old Elvis Presley hit, she thought, but
couldn't remember. She recognized some of the cus-
tomers—the couple who owned a small market
around the corner, a boy she'd stitched up when he'd
cracked his head inline skating, a young mother who
worked at the preschool where her twins were en-
rolled.

She ordered a diet cola for herself and milkshakes
for the girls, then waited nervously until she spied

Thorne push open one of the double glass doors. Tall, broad-shouldered, a determined expression on his bladed features, he glanced around the interior until his gaze landed full force on her. Her breath caught as if she were a silly schoolgirl and she mentally chided herself. *Get over it. He's just a man.* What was it about him that caused her idiotic heart to turn over at the sight of him? She waved and he strode through the maze of tables and booths.

"Where are—?" he started to ask before he spied the twins standing on chairs and peering over the shoulders of the boys working the video games. "Oh."

"They'll be back. I'm just lucky they don't understand they need money to work the machines."

"Then they'll break you."

"Exactly."

Hanging his leather jacket on a peg already holding one of the twins' coats, he glanced around the open restaurant, then slid onto the bench opposite her. "Not exactly what I had in mind when I called," he admitted, "but it'll do."

"Oh, will it?" she mocked.

"I haven't been here since high school."

"Fond memories?" She managed to keep her tone light though there had been times when she'd sat in this very booth hoping that Thorne McCafferty would call or return to Grand Hope. It hadn't happened.

"Some fonder than others." His gaze touched hers for a second. Picking up a plastic-coated menu, he elaborated, "I had the first date of my life here with Mary Lou Bennett when I was a freshman in high school. I was scared to death and then another

time—'' his eyes narrowed a fraction ''—I got into a
fight with a kid a couple of years older than me. What
was his name? A real tough…Mike something or
other…Wilkins…that was it. Mike Wilkins. He beat
the tar out of me in the parking lot.''

''He beat you up?''

''Yep. But I hate to admit it.'' He lifted an eyebrow. ''Oh, yes, Dr. Stevenson, I wasn't always the
tough guy you see before you.''

''What happened?'' she asked, fascinated. She'd
never heard this story before.

''The police came and hauled us both in. Took our
statements and those from the kids that had collected
around the fight. My dad had to come down and claim
me and I was nearly kicked out of school and thrown
off the football team, but, as usual, John Randall managed to pull some strings. The worst punishment I
ended up with was a black eye, a couple of loose teeth
and some pretty bad damage to my ego.''

''Which you probably deserved.''

''Probably.'' One side of his mouth lifted in a self-
deprecating grin. ''I was a little cocky.''

''Was?''

He snorted a laugh.

''What was the fight about?'' she asked, surprised
at his candor.

''What else? A girl. I was hitting on his girlfriend
and for the life of me I can't remember her name, but
she had red hair, a cute little smile and a few other
attributes as well.''

''And that's what attracted you—her 'attributes'?''

''And the fact that she was Mike Wilkins's girlfriend.'' His gray eyes twinkled. ''I've always liked

a challenge and a little competition never hurt, either.''

At that moment Molly came running up. ''I want a quarter.''

''Why?''

'''Cause that kid—'' she pointed an accusatory finger at a boy of eight or nine with spiky blond hair and freckles ''—he says I need one to play the games.''

Nicole shot Thorne a knowing look. ''Well, we don't have any time right now. Go and get your sister and let's order.''

''No!'' Molly's lower lip stuck out petulantly. ''I want a quarter.''

''Listen, not tonight, okay? Now, come on—'' Nicole glanced up at Thorne and sighed. ''Excuse me for a second, would you?'' She climbed out of the booth, made her way to the video machines and peeled Mindy from the chair on which she'd been standing. Mindy put up her kind of low-keyed fuss while Molly, ever more vocal, was bordering on being obnoxious.

''I want a quarter!'' she demanded, stomping her little foot imperiously.

''And I told you that we couldn't come here unless you behaved.'' Nicole managed to get both girls onto booster chairs, one on her side of the booth, the other next to Thorne.

''I want French fries,'' Molly stated.

''Oh, do you? Now there's a surprise.''

''And a hot dog.''

''Me, too,'' Mindy agreed. They managed to stay in their seats until the waitress, a slim teenaged girl in black slacks, crisp white shirt and red bow tie took their order. Then they were off again, making a bee-line for the video machines as the restaurant filled up and conversation buzzed through the air.

"See what you're in for?" Nicole's gaze followed her children. "I might have two the same age, but you'll have a newborn to deal with."

"Just until Randi can take over." He frowned and then settled back.

"I take it no one's been able to locate the baby's father?"

"Not yet. But we will." Determination pulled at the corners of his mouth.

She was disappointed that he seemed so anxious to cast off his responsibility of temporary father, but, as the waitress returned with their drink order, she reminded herself that he was, after all, a confirmed bachelor, a man more interested in making money than making babies.

Thorne noticed the play of emotions that crossed her face and the way her teasing smile suddenly disappeared.

"The reason I called you was that I need your help," he admitted. "We need a baby-sitter until Randi's well enough to take care of J.R."

"Oh."

He tried not to notice the sexy way her front teeth settled against her lower lip as she watched her girls, or the seductive way her blouse gaped at her neckline, showing off just the hint of cleavage. She glanced at him and in that second, when her gold eyes met his, he felt the incredible urge to kiss her again—just as he always did.

"It shouldn't be that hard to find someone suitable. I'm willing to pay whatever it takes."

"Money isn't the issue."

"Of course it is."

She rolled those expressive eyes and unwrapped her straw. "You still don't get it, do you? It's not about money." Taking a long sip from her soda she thought for a minute. "That's always been your problem, you know. Don't you understand that you can't go out and *buy* love? You can't expect to find the most loving, caring baby-sitter just by offering her a few more dollars. People are who they are. They don't change when you wave a check in front of their faces."

"I know that, but most people perform for money."

"You don't want someone to perform, you want someone who cares. There's a big difference. I'm not saying you don't pay them well, of course you do. But first you find the caring, warm, loving person. Then you pay them what they're worth to you."

"Is that what you did?"

"Absolutely. I located Jenny through an advertisement I ran in the local paper. After interviewing a dozen or so women and looking at day care centers, she called, we met and the rest is history. She's a part-time college student and the nicest woman you'd ever want to meet. She's warm, affectionate, wholesome and has a great sense of humor, which you need with kids. We work it out so that our schedules mesh. It takes some doing, but it can be accomplished." The waitress came with their trays of food and Thorne helped Nicole round up the girls. Just as they sat down, Nicole's pager went off. She glanced at the readout and frowned. "Look, I've got to make a call," she said. "I've got a cell phone out in the car— would you mind watching the girls just a minute?"

Thorne lifted a shoulder.

"No, Mommy," one of the twins cried.

"I'll be right back. Promise. Mr. McCafferty will help you open the ketchup packets for your French fries."

"Sure," Thorne said, though the thought of being with two four-year-old dynamos was a trifle daunting. Nicole slid out of the booth, then clipped across the tile floor. The twins looked ready to bolt after her, but Thorne distracted them with their milkshakes. He unwrapped their plastic straws then pushed them deep into their cups.

While one twin tried to suck up the milkshake the other was busy trying to open ketchup packages. Again he assisted and then squirted the red sauce over the fries. "Nooo!" the little girl wailed. "I want to dip!"

"What?"

"I want to dip. I don't want it on the top." Her little face was screwed up in a scowl as she glared at her basket. The other twin was sucking like crazy, trying to draw the too thick milkshake up her straw.

"It don't come," she complained.

"Just try harder."

"I am!"

"I don't like it," the first one insisted and Thorne seeing no other answer, took her hot dog, put it in his basket, then placed his cheeseburger in her basket and switched them. He handed her an opened packet of ketchup.

"You do it any way you want. Now—" he took the milkshake from the other girl's hands and opening in the lid, used the straw to swirl the chocolatey goo "—that should help," he said, replacing the lid and straw. "If it doesn't work, just give it a little time, it'll melt."

"Where's Mommy?" number one asked as she plopped a French fry into a pool of ketchup that she'd created.

"In the car making a call."

"Is she coming back?"

"I think so," he said and winked. The pixies tore into their food, pulling off the buns and squeezing more mustard and ketchup onto their hot dogs than was necessary but Thorne, not used to being around children of any age, decided to let them do what they wanted. By the time Nicole returned, they had condiments on their faces, hands, clothes and even in their hair.

"Everything all right?" he asked.

"Minor emergency—nothing serious. I handled it. Oh, what happened?" she asked, eyeing her daughters.

"They ate."

"Didn't they give you bibs?" Her eyes fell to the tray where two plastic bibs were tucked.

"Didn't see 'em."

Sighing, she wiped one face, then the other before finally turning her attention to her own dinner. "You have a lot to learn," she said, biting into her hamburger.

"That's why I need a nanny."

"Or two," she said.

"As I mentioned, I was hoping you could help me out in that department."

"How?"

"Either you or your sitter might be able to give me the names of people who would be interested in a part-time or full-time job taking care of the baby. At least until Randi's on her feet and able to care for him."

"It's a possibility," she said, touching a napkin to the corner of her lips, then automatically wiping a smudge from one of her daughter's cheeks.

"Don't!" the little girl cried.

"Oh, Molly, don't be such a grump." Nicole was undeterred and soon, despite much cringing and grumbling, the little girl's face was condiment-free and they were all digging into their food again.

Thorne watched Nicole with her daughters, how she joked with them and played with them even when she was disciplining them. She didn't raise her voice, always paid attention when they spoke and pointed out their mistakes with a wink and a smile. It didn't always work. The precocious one challenged her mother and the shier little girl sometimes didn't speak and offered Nicole a cold shoulder, but throughout the meal one thing was clear—Nicole Sanders Stevenson, M.D. was one helluva mother.

Not that it mattered. He wasn't looking for a woman who could raise children. Hell, he wasn't even looking for a woman period.

Yet, for a reason he couldn't name he still carried that damned ring his father had given him in his pocket.

Chapter Twelve

Thorne had never felt so awkward in his life. He'd just fed the baby and burped him and heard soft little sighs against his shoulder as he walked from the den to the living room and wondered how the hell he was going to get J.R. into his crib without waking him. The baby, bright-eyed and healthy, seemed the most content while being held, which was a worry.

A natural athlete, Thorne had been able to handle a wet football, rope a calf, ride a horse, or crack a baseball over the fence, but when it came to holding, feeding, burping and diapering a tiny infant, he was all thumbs.

Not that his brothers were any better at it. Matt had spent his life on the ranch and had dealt with everything from newly hatched chicks to orphaned lambs and foals who were rejected by the mares that gave them birth. He'd helped bring litters of puppies and kittens into this world. But when it came to helpless human babies, he, too, seemed out of place and incompetent. Slade was the worst. Although fascinated beyond belief with the baby, he seemed terrified to hold J.R. That part was downright ridiculous in Thorne's estimation, though Matt was amused that his daredevil of a brother was frightened of the infant.

J.R.'s eyes blinked open.

Uh-oh.

Within seconds he started to put up a fuss and Thorne tried not to panic. "You're all right," he said, wondering how it was that mothers seemed to have some kind of natural rhythm while holding and swaying slightly as they held a child. He'd seen that same natural reaction through the glass window of the hospital when Nicole had cradled and fed the baby.

He tried to sway, felt like an ass and the baby started crying in earnest, wailing and turning red in the face. "Now, it's okay," Thorne reassured the child when he had no idea whatsoever was wrong with him. "Hang in there."

Juanita's footsteps echoed down the stairs. "I'm coming, I'm coming," she said to Thorne's utter relief.

A second later she appeared. "He is tired."

"He *was* asleep."

"Then why didn't you put him in his *cuna?*"

"Because I couldn't get to his *cuna,*" Thorne said, emphasizing the Spanish word, "without waking him up."

"But you woke him up anyway." She lifted a gray-

ing eyebrow as the baby cried louder than Thorne
thought was possible.

"Believe me, I wasn't trying to."

"Here, let me have him. Come on, little one," she
said softly, prying him from Thorne's stiff fingers.
She began to murmur softly in Spanish as she carried
the infant from the room and to Thorne's mortification the baby started to quiet. Within minutes silence
prevailed and Juanita, walking softly, returned.

"How do you do that?"

"Practice," she said and smiled.

"Maybe I need lessons."

"*Dios,* all you brothers do. And probably Señorita
Randi as well. How is she going to take care of the
baby, write her columns, finish her book and get
well?" She shook her head as she headed to the
kitchen.

"There is no book," Thorne said, following her
down the hallway. "Remember, that was always just
her dream. Nothing ever came of it."

"But she said that she would write one. I believed
it. She will be rich and famous one day. You will
see." She scrounged in the refrigerator, muttered
something under her breath and reached inside where
she found a package, opened it and looked at Harold
who lay on a rag rug near the back door. "I saved
this soup bone for you," she told him as the crippled
dog climbed to his feet and wagged his tail. "But you
take it outside." She tossed the bone to the dog and
looked over her shoulder at Thorne. "There is a
book."

"I hope so," Thorne said, but nearly dismissed the
idea. Randi had talked about writing the Great Amer-

ican Novel ever since she was fifteen. To his knowl-
edge she hadn't written the first sentence much less a
chapter or two. There was nothing to it, he told himself, but made a mental note to mention Randi's pipe
dream to Striker. Why not? It certainly wouldn't hurt.

Nicole climbed out of the bathtub and stepped into
her robe. The twins were asleep, the house quiet.
Cinching the belt, she padded to the kitchen and
heated a cup of cocoa. Patches, curled on a cushion
of one of the café chairs at the table, opened one eye
and yawned, showing off needle-sharp teeth before
resting his chin on his paws again. The microwave
dinged and Nicole picked up her cup to carry into the
living room where a fire still burned in the grate. Scarlet coals glowed brightly and the fire popped and
hissed.

Sipping from her cup, Nicole settled into a corner
of her love seat and flipped through a parenting magazine. She'd just started reading an article on a toddler's stages of life when she noticed the column—
advice for the single parent, written by R. J. McKay.
Why it caught her eye, she didn't know, but she began
reading the text and an eerie sensation crawled up her
spine. It was written with a light hand and ironic style
that was identical to that in the columns she'd read
by Randi McCafferty. But no one had ever mentioned
that Randi had expanded her column from newspa-
pers to magazines. Not that it wasn't common.

She sipped her cocoa and started rereading the article when she heard a vehicle ease down the street.
The engine slowed, then died in front of her house

and when she twisted to peek through the blinds she spied Thorne striding up her front walk.

Her pulse leaped at the sight of him and then she remembered that she was wearing only her robe. On her feet in an instant, she started for the bedroom just as she heard the doorbell ring.

"Damn." She hesitated then walked back to the door and swung it open. Wind ruffled his hair and billowed her skirt as it swept into the room. "Well, Mr. McCafferty, this is a surprise."

A cocksure smile stretched across his lips as his gaze traveled the length of her. "A good one, I hope."

"That depends," she teased, unable to stop herself.

"On?"

"You, of course."

He didn't wait. In half a heartbeat he crossed the threshold, his arms were around her and his cold lips found hers. Icy wind swirled around them and just before she closed her eyes and he kicked the door shut, she saw the first few snowflakes fall from the night-dark heavens.

But the snowfall was instantly forgotten. The pressure of his lips was insistent and her heart went wild, pounding out of control, thundering in her ears.

Warmth invaded her limbs and desire slowly uncoiled deep within her. He backed her against the foyer's wall and she willingly complied, winding her arms around his neck, parting her lips, thrilling to the cool, welcome touch of his skin against hers. He smelled of the outdoors—pine laced with the traces of some musky cologne. His body was hard, tense muscles strong as they pressed intimately against hers. This was a mistake. She knew it, but couldn't resist the sweet seduction of his touch, the tingle his lips evoked.

His hands found her belt and as if he had all the time in the world he continued to kiss her as he loosened the knot. His tongue touched hers, flicking and tasting, causing her head to swim. She could barely breathe as her robe parted and with cold, callused fingers he lifted one breast in his hand. Her nipple puckered expectantly and deep inside she turned liquid.

"Oh, Nicole," he murmured against the shell of her ear. Desire was throbbing through her and emotions she didn't pause to understand raced through her mind. "We're alone?" His voice was low and husky.

"No." She shook her head and had trouble finding her voice. Lust pulsed through her veins. "The twins are here."

"Asleep?"

She nodded as his fingers scraped along the front lapel of her robe, touching her skin so lightly she wanted to scream. "It's...it's all right," she said though she wasn't thinking clearly, couldn't concentrate on anything but the want of him.

"Good." He kissed her again and reaching down, placed an arm beneath her knees and lifted her from her feet. As if she were nearly weightless he carried her down the short hallway past the girls' room to her bedroom—a private sanctuary where, heretofore, no man had ever been allowed to enter.

Somehow he managed to close and lock the door before placing her on the bed. Beneath her old hand-pieced quilt, the mattress sagged under their com-

bined weight. "Wh-what's got into you?" she asked
as he pushed the robe off her shoulders.

He stopped, his hands unmoving for a second as
his silvery gaze found hers. "You, Doctor." He
leaned forward and kissed her slowly on the lips.
"You've gotten into me and I can't seem to do anything about it but this."

"Would you want to?" she asked and smiled.

"No." He parted the robe and took both her breasts
in his hands. Holding them together he kissed the tops
of each before guiding her fingers to his shirt. She
needed no further instruction and began to remove his
jacket, sweater and jeans while he never stopped kissing her, touching her, or causing her blood to heat
and the yearning deep within her most private of
regions to become ever more insistent.

Don't do this, that nagging little voice in her head
screamed, but she ignored it.

His fingers tangled in her hair, then moved down
her back, kneading and probing. His body molded to
hers. He tasted of salt and desire and she wanted him
as she'd never wanted another man.

Only he could satisfy her.

Only he could send her soaring to heights she'd
only imagined. She kissed him and dug her fingers
into his shoulders.

Anxious, strident muscles rubbed against her softer,
yielding flesh. His tongue found and rimmed the hollow of her throat before seeking darker, deeper clefts
that made her bite her lip to keep from screaming out.
Intimate spasms erupted deep inside before he came
to her, parting her legs, kissing her and holding her
close. She arched upward, wanting more, needing re-

lease. "Thorne—" she whispered when she thought
she'd go mad with desire "—Thorne, for the love
of—oh, oooh."

With one forceful thrust he began to make love to
her then and didn't stop. As her breathing became
shallow and her body sheened with a layer of perspiration, he kissed her, loved her. Over and over he
claimed her until the first streaks of daylight pierced
through the window shades and she, exhausted, still
holding him close, finally drifted off.

The girls awakened a few hours later and the bed
was cold and empty, only the faint scent of sex lingering with the sweet, sensual memories of lovemaking stealing through her mind. She glanced at the bureau where the rose he'd given her had faded and
died, the petals falling onto the old wood. She hadn't
thrown the flower out; couldn't.

She was tired, yes, but felt better than she had in
years. She sang in the shower, laughed when the girls
fought, dressed with a smile on her face. It was only
when she was yanking a brush through her hair that
she caught a glimpse of her reflection, and she noticed
the curve of her lips and the sparkle in her eyes. "Oh,
no," she said, disbelieving.

But she couldn't deny the plain truth that stared her
squarely in the face: she was, despite all her warnings
to herself, falling head over heels in love with Thorne
McCafferty.

Denver held no appeal to him. His apartment
seemed as cold and empty as an ice cave and though
it was clean, every surface shining, fresh towels hung
over the brass towel bars, a lit fire at his fingertips,

he felt no sense of homecoming. His closet was filled with suits, sport coats, slacks and three tuxedos; the view from his living room and master bedroom, a spectacular array of the lights of the city. And yet he felt as if he were in a foreign land, an alien in a penthouse that he'd called home for more years than he wanted count.

He'd arrived in town in the morning and gone straight to the office. Somehow he'd survived four meetings before driving here where he intended to change and attend the black-tie affair hosted by Kent Williams. The dinner was for a charitable cause but the business behind the scenes was all about turning a profit. Not that he minded. Thorne was the first man to admit to being interested in making money.

And yet...

He poured himself a glass of Scotch and stared out the panorama of windows. Snow was falling and the lights of the city winked through the veil of flakes. He saw his own reflection in the glass, a tall man in a slightly wrinkled suit, holding a drink he didn't want and feeling more alone than he ever had in his life.

He'd never been one to dislike his own company; in fact, he'd silently laughed at men who needed a woman on their arms, showpieces, accessories, or even wives they adored. It had all seemed so weak and cowardly; but now, as he looked at that pale, distorted, ghostlike image of himself in the window, he imagined Nicole with him. Whether dressed in a sequined evening gown, or a pair of jeans and tennis shoes, or a lab coat over slacks and a blouse, her image seemed perfect at his side.

"Idiot," he muttered and tossed back his drink. He'd go to the damned party, do his business and drive to the airport tonight. The weather service was predicting two feet of snow to be dumped on the Denver area in the next couple of days, but Thorne intended to return to Grand Hope as soon as he could escape the obligations of his position.

There were too many pressing problems in Montana for him to tarry in this soulless suite he'd once considered home.

Home. Ha!

What were all the old sayings?

Home sweet home?

There's no place like home?

Home is where the heart is?

He took one final look around the living room as he strode to the bedroom to dig out one of his tuxedos. One thing was for certain: his heart wasn't here. Nope—it was currently residing in the hallways of St. James Hospital with the stubborn, bright, beautiful emergency room physician he'd once turned his back on—a divorced woman with two children already and no apparent desire to settle down again.

Well, all that was about to change. Thorne was used to taking charge of a situation, of getting what he wanted, and right now as he pulled out the designer tux with the forest-green cummerbund, he wanted Dr. Nicole Stevenson. One way or another he'd have her.

Nicole was dead on her feet. She'd worked overtime as there was a horrible accident involving two cars and a pickup. The wreck had occurred just two miles outside the city limits of Grand Hope. An eighty-year-old man and a teenager hadn't survived; the man's wife and three other teenagers were fighting for their lives. All were in critical condition with head injuries, punctured lungs, cracked ribs, ruptured spleens and all manner of contusions. A middle-aged housewife and her two children that were in the pickup had survived with only minor injuries, but the ER had been a madhouse and every available doctor, nurse, aid and anesthesiologist had been called in. Only now, ten hours after the first ambulance had arrived and they'd dealt with the severely injured, were things finally settling down. The rest of the patients, a woman who had scalded herself, an eight-year-old who had slammed his finger in a car door, three flu cases and a man complaining of dizzy spells had been forced to wait.

But the worst of the chaos was over, the patients stabilized, and relief physicians had arrived. Finally, Nicole could go home. She poured herself a fresh cup of coffee and quickly wrote some notes on her computer before grabbing her jacket, laptop and briefcase and leaving St. James.

The parking lot was a blanket of white as snow had fallen all day long. Six inches had piled in the parking lot and ice and snow had collected on the SUV's windshield. She waited for the defroster and wipers to clear the glass, then drove carefully into town.

She hadn't heard from Thorne since yesterday morning and she was beginning to miss him, though she didn't want to admit how deeply and emotionally entangled she'd become with him and his entire family.

"Oh, don't be a fool," she told herself as she stopped to ease the rig into four-wheel drive. She decided to call Thorne when she got home, tell him about a friend of Jenny's who was interested in the nanny job and just reconnect. After all, in these days of women's liberation, why couldn't she call him rather than sit by the phone or wonder what he was doing?

She made her way home and found her girls already dressed in their pajamas and ready for bed. "Sorry I'm late," she apologized to Jenny after hugging each twin and listening to them babble on about what they'd done during the day. There was talk of a snowman in the backyard and Mindy complained that Molly had hit her with a snowball.

"Did not!" Molly cried, but guilt contorted her little face and she called her sister a tattletale when she finally confessed without a drop of remorse.

"They've been pretty good," Jenny admitted and hugged each girl before leaving. With the twins standing on the love seat, their noses pressed to the window, Nicole watched as Jenny drove off through the storm, the taillights of her battle-scarred station wagon winking bright red against a shower of snowflakes.

It was nearly two hours later, once Molly and Mindy were fast asleep, that she dialed the number of the Flying M. The phone was answered by a woman with a thick Spanish accent.

"McCafferty Ranch."

"This is Nicole Stevenson. I'm looking for—"

"The doctor. *Dios!* Has something happened to Señorita Randi?"

"No, I just wanted to talk to Thorne."

"But Randi, she is the same?"

"Yes. As far as I know."

There was a heavy sigh on the other end of the line. "Thorne, he is not here, but you can speak to Slade."

Disappointment pierced her soul. "No, that's all right. Have Thorne give me a call when he returns."

"He is not coming back for a while," the woman said, then holding her hand over the receiver spoke to someone else and within a few seconds Slade's voice boomed over the wires.

"Is this Nicole?"

"Yes."

There was a moment's hesitation. "Oh. Well, I thought you knew. Thorne's in Denver. We don't expect him back for a few days. We're not really sure but the storm's hit hard there and it looks like he won't be back for a while—uh-oh." In the background she heard a baby start to put up a fuss. "Was there a message I could pass along to him?"

"No, not really," she said, feeling deflated somehow. "I thought he was looking for a nanny and I have the number of a woman who might be a possibility."

The baby was really wailing by this time. "Great. The job hasn't been filled yet. Why don't you give me the information?"

"Sure. The woman's name is Christina Foster." She gave Slade Christina's number and was about to hang up when she remembered something she'd wanted to tell Thorne but hadn't had the chance. "You know, Slade, I was reading an article in a magazine the other night. It was about single parenting and the byline was for an R. J. McKay. I know this sounds crazy, but it sure read like something your sister might have written.''

''Is that so?'' Slade was all ears. ''You still got a copy of it?''

''Yes.''

''I'd like to see it.''

''Sure, but as I said, I'm not certain it was written by Randi.''

''Nonetheless.''

''I'll make you a copy and send it to you.''

''Thanks.''

She hung up and felt a big case of the blues threatening to overtake her. So Thorne was in Denver. So what?

Why didn't he mention that he was going? Why hasn't he called?

''Stop it,'' she told herself. She *wasn't* going to be one of those women who sat around and stewed over a man. No way, no how. And yet, as she pulled the blinds and saw one last view of the snowy night, she couldn't help wish that Thorne was here with her, holding her in his arms and making love to her as if he would never stop.

Cradling a cup of coffee, Thorne glowered out the window to the gray morning. Snow was still falling as if it would never stop and the airport was a mess. At another time in his life, he would have kept busy, gone to the office, buried himself in his work, managed his life around the natural disaster that seemed hell-bent on causing him problems. But now he wanted to return to Grand Hope, Montana—to the ranch, to Randi, to little J.R. and especially to Nicole. Grand Hope was where he belonged. With his brothers and sister. With his nephew. With the woman he loved.

Silently he sipped his black coffee and laughed at himself. Thorne McCafferty, once upon a time a confirmed bachelor, now contemplating not just living with a woman for the rest of his life, but marrying her.

Matt and Slade would needle him mercilessly when they found out. But he didn't mind.

His head still ached from the buzz of last night's party. Kent Williams had been attentive and brought several ideas to him—a condominium project in Aspen, single-family courtyard homes in a development just outside of Denver, and an apartment complex in Boulder. He'd been certain they could work something out and all the while Annette had hovered near him, touching him, smiling up at him, showing off her sleek body in a low-cut gown of mauve silk while he spoke to other businessmen and reporters who were covering the event. She'd even managed to loop her arm through his while a society page reporter had spoken with him and a photographer had flashed his picture.

Thorne hadn't been interested in her advances, but had managed to smile and accept her attentions throughout the night. Only when he was leaving and she suggested that she was available to come to his place for drinks did he pull her into a private alcove of the hotel and tell her in no uncertain terms that it was over. When she'd pouted, he'd had to tell her that he was involved with another woman. She hadn't believed him and had thrown her arms around his neck and tried to kiss him. Only then, when he hadn't responded, had she realized that he was serious.

"I just hope whoever she is she knows what she's got in you," she'd said icily. "No woman with any heart wants a man married to his work."

He hadn't responded but had silently thought that Nicole didn't even know he loved her; would probably reject him when he proposed. At that thought he smiled for the first time in twenty-four hours. The memory of making love to her had lingered in his mind, but that wasn't all of it. Their lovemaking was wild, raw and passionate, but sex wasn't the driving force. No, he loved Nicole the concerned physician, Nicole the tenderhearted mother, Nicole the brassy woman who stood up to him and joked with him as well as Nicole the sexy lady he wanted to forever warm his bed.

So he was stuck in Denver. Great. He might as well make the most of it. He decided to go into the office, do as much work as he could while he was here and then as soon as the weather broke, he would fly back to the pine-forested slopes of Montana where he belonged.

He showered, changed into a business suit that felt strangely uncomfortable, then he walked the few blocks through the snow-crusted streets to the office. He spent the next hour with Eloise who brought him up to date on his projects. "You know," she said, checking off another item on her list as she sat on one side of his desk and he on the other. "This is working better than I thought."

"What is?"

"You being at the ranch in Montana. I have to admit that I thought it was a crazy scheme when you came up with it."

"The art of telecommunications."

"I suppose."

"Or maybe you just like being in charge when I'm gone."

"Oh, yeah, that's it." A twinkle lit her eyes. "Okay, is there anything else?"

"Yes, get me a florist on the line would you?"

"You want me to send flowers for you?"

Thorne leaned back in his chair. "No, this time I'll handle it personally."

"Uh-oh. Someone special?"

"Very." He leaned back in his chair and noticed the shocked expression on his secretary's face. "Very special to me."

"Will do." She left his office, buzzed him a few minutes later and told him the florist was on line two. Thorne pulled at his collar and told the man on the other end of the line what he wanted and when he was finished, he grinned widely. That should knock the lady doc's socks off.

The intercom buzzed insistently and when he picked up, Eloise told him that a man named Kurt Striker was on hold.

"Put him through." There was a click. "Striker?"

"Yep. Listen, you told me to let you know if I found out anything about your sister's accident."

All the muscles in the back of Thorne's neck contracted. "I remember."

"Well, I've done some pokin' around."

"And?"

"I think that your sister's accident involved another vehicle—a maroon Ford product, from the looks of it. Either that rig edged her off the road on purpose or clipped her fender, sent her reeling and the driver got so scared he didn't bother to stop. The least it could be is a hit-and-run accident, the worst case scenario is attempted murder."

Thorne's heart turned to stone. A tic developed over his eye.

"You're sure about this?"

"Yep," Striker said, his voice as strong as steel. "I'd be willing to bet my life on it."

Chapter Thirteen

"I guess when your name is McCafferty, there's no way you can keep it away from the press." Maureen Oliverio slapped a copy of the newspaper down on the table and slid into a chair in the cafeteria where Nicole was finishing her lunch.

"Don't tell me, some reporter is writing about Randi again."

"Not just Randi, but the whole damned family." Maureen opened a packet of nondairy creamer and poured the white powder into her cup of coffee. "Page three."

Nicole pushed her cup of soup aside and spread the paper open. As she did, her heart nearly stopped. Yes, there was an article about the McCaffertys and Randi's accident, but the text was more in-depth and gave an overview of John Randall McCafferty, who

had once been so influential in the area surrounding
Grand Hope. There was also a sketchy story of what
his children were doing. There were old snapshots of
the McCafferty brothers playing football, a picture of
Slade after his skiing accident, a shot of Matt riding
rodeo and another picture, one taken just the day before, if the date was to be believed, of Thorne at a
charitable fund-raiser in Denver. On his arm was a
striking woman who positively glowed in her designer gown and diamonds.

Nicole's world spun for a second. Her throat closed
and she tried to deny what was so obvious. Then,
gritting her teeth and finding a scrap of her self-
esteem she scanned the article before lifting her eyes
and reading the concern in Maureen's gaze. "I don't
know what possessed me to buy this," the emergency
room team leader said, "but I thought you'd like to
see it."

"Yes. Thank you." No words were spoken but a
moment of understanding passed between them. Maureen wouldn't embarrass her by stating the obvious:
that Thorne was dating other women while he was
seeing Nicole, and Nicole didn't have to make excuses or defend him. The thread of friendship—the
woman-bond—between Maureen and Nicole ran too
deep for that kind of false pride. They were more than
colleagues, more than friends. They belonged to an
unspoken sisterhood of single women raising families.

"You can have it."

"Good."

Her pager went off and Nicole read the message—

a code that she needed to be in the ER. At the same time Maureen's beeper caught her attention.

"Gotta run," Nicole said.

"Me, too. I'll meet you in the ER."

On her feet in an instant, Nicole tucked the damning newspaper under her arm. What did she expect? Of course Thorne dated other women. He probably had one in every city where he did work. The thought made her stomach turn over. Why, oh, for the love of God, why did she let herself fall in love with him?

At the elevators Nicole gave herself a quick mental shake. She couldn't be worrying about Thorne or wondering about him or pining over him. She had work to do. Important work. She climbed onto the elevator car, pushed the button for the main floor and once on ground level, swept through the doors to the ER.

"What've we got?" she asked, pulling on a pair of disposable gloves as Maureen appeared through a side door. Tension crackled in the air.

"Plane crash, just outside of town. Some idiot was trying to fly a private jet in this mess," a nurse said as she hung up the phone. "Close enough that he's coming in by ambulance."

"How many injured?" Nicole asked.

"Just the pilot, I think."

"And he's alive?"

"As far as I know."

"Lucky stiff."

At that moment the sound of sirens split the air. "Okay, people, let's get to work!"

The ambulance, siren screaming, roared into the parking lot. Tires and chains squealed. Two paramed-

ics flew out of the back. A police car—lights flashing
in red and blue—skidded in behind the ambulance.
As the patient was wheeled inside, two deputies from
the sheriff's department stormed in.

"What have we got here?" Nicole asked.

"Thirty-nine-year-old man, unconscious, head injuries, broken femur, blood pressure stable at…"

The paramedic rambled on and Nicole heard the
vital signs, but her heart was thundering, her legs
weak as she stared into the mangled face of the patient and knew, before anyone said a word, that this
was Thorne. The overhead lights seemed brighter and
started to swim in her eyes. Her heart pounded in her
ears and she couldn't breathe. Her legs threatened to
give out and she braced herself against the wall.

"Who is he?"

"Thorne McCafferty," she heard through her fog
and forced her eyes into the serious gaze of a woman
deputy from the sheriff's department. Her name tag
read Detective Kelly Dillinger.

"Oh, God," she whispered. "No. No. Oh, God,
no—"

"I'll take over," Maureen said from somewhere
behind her and the room began to go dark. "Nicole.
I said—"

"No, I'll be all right." Her fingers wrapped around
the cold metal railing of the gurney as she turned to
face Maureen.

"I'll handle it, *Doctor*." Behind the understanding
in Maureen's eyes, was an insistence that warned Nicole she would hear of no argument. Several nurses
were staring. All the while Thorne lay still, needing

assistance. "You're too involved emotionally, and I'm the team leader," Maureen pointed out.

"All right." Nicole had no choice but to back down. She was shaking and needed to pull herself together. "But as soon as you've examined him, let me know. I'll be in my office and I'll call his family."

"Fine." All business, Maureen Oliverio nodded. "Talk to the detective and I'll see to the patient. Let's go!"

As she watched helplessly, Thorne was wheeled into an examining room.

"What did she mean you were too involved?" the detective asked.

With pale skin and piercing brown eyes she stared at Nicole from beneath the brim of her hat. A few wisps of red hair feathered around her face.

"I—I know the family."

"And Thorne McCafferty specifically?"

"Yes. He and I have dated," she admitted, finally coming to grips with the situation. Her spine found some starch and she was no longer quivering inside but she suspected her face was pale as death. "He's a friend of mine. What happened?" As she talked she peeled off her gloves and tossed them into a waste receptacle.

"His plane went down in the storm and we're investigating the cause of the accident. Probably just the weather, but we have to be sure." Detective Dillinger's lips pursed a bit. "He's lucky to be alive."

Nicole glanced to the examining room and nodded. To think that Thorne might have lost his life. Oh, God. What then? Her heart ached at the thought of it.

She cleared her throat and saw a news van wheel into the lot. "Uh-oh."

Looking over her shoulder, the detective recognized the van. Her lips tightened into a frown of disapproval. She nodded to her partner and ordered, "Handle the vultures. And don't tell them the name of the pilot until we talk to his family."

"Got it." The other officer, a lanky man in his early twenties blocked the entrance. The reporter, a petite woman in a bright-blue coat argued as a wiry cameraman stared through the glass.

"Can we talk somewhere a little more private?" Detective Dillinger asked and for the first time Nicole was aware of the curious stares that were cast in her direction.

"Yeah—my office, just let me tell the staff where to reach me." Another doctor agreed to take over for the next half hour while Nicole managed to rein in her wild emotions and escorted the detective upstairs to her office.

"Have a seat," Nicole offered, snatching a stack of books off the chair. She set the books on an empty corner of her desk and settled into her own seat.

"I know this is tough on you right now, and I wouldn't bother you, but since you're close to the McCafferty family maybe you can give me some information."

"As soon as I alert his brothers," Nicole said, her head finally clear again. Somehow she had to put her own emotions aside and don her facade of professionalism, not only for herself, but for Thorne as well. Her fingers were still slightly unsteady, but she picked up the phone. "Matt and Slade need to know that their brother's been in an accident and admitted to St. James.'' She didn't wait for a response, just dialed the ranch and gave the message to Slade, who shocked, didn't say a word until she was finished.

Then he swore a blue streak. ''Damn it all, how can this happen? What kind of a fool gets into a plane in the middle of a blizzard?'' he asked, then sighed loudly. ''I guess it doesn't matter. Just tell me. Is he gonna make it?''

''Yes—I think so.'' The thought of Thorne giving up his life was too painful to consider. She cleared her throat and was aware of the detective's eyes silently assessing her and her reaction. ''A team of our best doctors is working to stabilize him in the emergency room. From there he'll see specialists.''

''Son of a—'' Slade began, and then shouted in another direction. ''Juanita, can you watch the baby for a while? Thorne's been in an accident and he's at the hospital.''

''Dios!'' the woman cried. ''This family, it has a *maldición!''*

''There is no curse, Juanita.'' Slade's voice was muffled but firm. ''Will you watch—''

''Sí, sí! I will stay.''

''I'll round up Matt,'' Slade said into the mouthpiece. ''We'll be there as soon as we can.'' He hung up and Nicole, still shaken, slowly set down the receiver. Once again, she found herself staring into the scrutinizing gaze of Detective Kelly Dillinger.

''They're on their way?'' she asked.

''Both Matt and Slade.''

''Good.''

''What is it you want to know?''

"Just a little family history," the detective said, pulling out a notepad. "The reason is simple. First the sister is nearly killed in an accident, has a baby who nearly doesn't make it, remains comatose and leaves a lot of questions unanswered. We can't contact the baby's father as no one seems to know who he is, and we can't talk to her and find out why her car went out of control."

"I thought she hit ice," Nicole said, a needle of dread piercing her heart.

"She did. But the family's insistent that there was another vehicle involved. They hired an independent investigator who's determined to prove that there was some kind of foul play." She took off her hat and red hair spilled around her face in soft layers. "Okay, that's what some families do. It makes them feel better—to pay someone to dig deeper than the police. Or so they think."

"But—was there? Foul play?"

"We don't know," the detective said, her face without expression, her eyes serious. "But I'm trying to find out." She clicked her pen a couple of times, then jotted a quick note. "I wasn't convinced that there was anything to go on, but now there's been another accident involving another member of the family, so I guess I'm just covering all bases."

"But the plane crash, it was an accident." It had to have been. No one would try to harm Thorne—to *murder* him!

"Most likely it was an accident. The storm was bad and those light planes…well…" She cocked her head to one side. "But if it's all just coincidence, then this McCafferty family is having one string of bad luck.

If not...then maybe that P.I. knows something the sheriff's department doesn't. I'm here to figure it out.''

Nicole's head pounded. Was this possible? Someone out to hurt the McCafferty clan? She swallowed hard and refused to give in to that kind of fear. So far no one had proved anything other than the fact that there had been some accidents. Bad luck, that was it. It had to be.

She checked her watch. Thorne had been in the ER for over thirty minutes. Surely someone knew the extent of his injuries by now. Yet no one had called and she was edgy, her nerves strung tight as piano wires. What if something had gone wrong? Distracted, she tried to answer as many questions as possible and talked with the detective for a few more minutes before she explained that she really had to go back to work.

''That's fine. I'll need to speak to the patient when he wakes up,'' Kelly Dillinger said, ''and I'll want to talk to his brothers.'' She scraped her chair back, grabbed her hat and together they took the elevator down to the emergency room. The detective hurried out to her police car and Nicole was immediately immersed in her work.

Nicole saw three more patients, a seven-year-old girl who needed five stitches to her forehead after being hit by the end of a twirling baton that had lost its rubber tip and had been wielded by her younger brother, a septuagenarian with a mild case of bronchitis, and an ashen-faced teenager who thought she had a bad case of the flu and showed shock, then horror when tests confirmed that she was nearly three months' pregnant.

By the time Nicole had finished the examinations, the ER was clear. She talked to the nurses and found out that Thorne had been admitted. He was stable and aside from a few contusions and a broken leg that would require surgery once the swelling had gone down, he was healthy.

"Thank God," she whispered as she made her way to his private room. Matt and Slade were camped out at his bedside. Both men wore deep frowns and their eyes were dark with worry.

"I can't believe it," Slade muttered as he walked to the hallway and reached into the inside pocket of his jacket for a crumpled pack of cigarettes. He retrieved the pack, then realized what he was doing and returned it to his pocket. "What in the hell is going on?" He shot an angry glance at Nicole. "Now we got two in this hospital again! The baby just got home and Thorne winds up here!"

"He's going to make it, though. Okay?" Matt muttered. "That's something."

"Damned fool! What was he doin' flyin' in that storm?" Slade closed his eyes and pinched the bridge of his nose as if trying to stave off a headache.

"He thought he should get back—"

Slade's eyes flew open and he dropped his hand only to raise a finger and jab it at Matt's chest. "Because he doesn't have any faith that we can handle the ranch, or the baby or Randi's situation, ourselves. He's got no faith in anyone but himself! A control freak. That's what he is. A damned, corporate control freak."

"Enough!" Matt's face had turned a deep shade of scarlet. "This isn't getting us anywhere."

"I'm going to tell Striker." Slade rammed his fingers through his hair and as if a sudden thought had struck him, turned all of his attention in Nicole's direction. "You said you had some article that Randi might have written?"

"I took a copy and sent it to you."

"Hell, I didn't even think of the mail today." He rubbed the back of his neck in frustration.

"Have you talked to anyone from the sheriff's department?" Nicole asked.

"The sheriff's department?" Matt's eyes narrowed. "Why?"

"They're investigating the accident. I spoke with a Detective Dillinger and she said she wants to talk to you."

"Because—?" Matt asked, but the look in his eyes convinced Nicole that he already knew the answer.

"Because finally someone's starting to believe what Kurt Striker has been saying all along," Slade answered. "I'm going to call him right now."

"And I'll talk to the police." Matt's jaw was hard as granite. "If this isn't just an accident, I'm going to find out who's behind it." He squared his hat onto his head. "You'll call me if there's a change in Thorne's condition?"

"Of course."

As the brothers strode down the hall together, Nicole entered Thorne's darkened room. She told herself that she saw injured people all the time, victims who had suffered horrid accidents and disfigurements, that she could stomach anything. But seeing Thorne lying inert beneath the crisp bedsheets, with an IV running into the back of his hand, his leg elevated in a temporary cast, his face cut and swollen beyond recognition, each breath seeming labored, her heart nearly broke.

"Oh, honey," she whispered, her throat closing in on itself. She loved him. God, how she loved him and he'd betrayed her; been with another woman. She licked her lips and fought tears. There he lay, a broken leg, a concussion, his head bandaged, his features barely recognizable. "I'm sorry it didn't work out," she said, her voice a rasp, her fingers touching the tips of his. "I did love you. Oh, Thorne, if you only knew how much." Sniffing a bit, she cleared her throat. "But then I always was a fool over you. I suppose I always will be." His eyelids didn't so much as flutter. "You get better, y'hear? I'll be back and, damn it, if you do something foolish like take a turn for the worse, I swear, I'll kill you myself." She laughed a bit at her own stupid joke and realized that tears were falling from her eyes. "Oh, look at this. I'm such a moron. *You* make me a moron. I, uh, I've got to go check on the girls." She dabbed at her eyes with a tissue she found near the bedside. "But I'll be back. I promise." She leaned over the bed and placed a kiss on his forehead, leaving a lipstick smudge and a tearstain that she quickly brushed aside. "You know, Thorne," she confided, "I was foolish enough to want to spend the rest of my life with you."

She waited, half expecting him to respond, silently praying there would be a squeeze on her fingers, rapid eye movement behind his closed lids, even the barest change in his breathing, but she was disappointed.

Like his sister in ICU, Thorne heard nothing and didn't so much as flinch.

Nicole left the room with a weight as heavy as all Montana pressing down her shoulders. She wrote her notes in a daze, then grabbed her coat, changed into boots and headed home. Outside the snow was still flurrying, swirling and dancing across the frozen landscape. In gloves and a down ski jacket, she turned the radio and heater on full blast, but couldn't thaw the ice in her soul at the thought of Thorne's plane crash and how close he'd come to losing his life.

And how would you feel then? If he'd died or was in serious risk of losing his life? Or paralyzed for the rest of his life?

She shuddered and tried to concentrate on a song playing through the speakers, but the lyrics of false love scraped too close to the bone. Angrily, she snapped off the radio. She was no longer involved with Thorne. He wanted it that way. It had been a mistake to get involved with him again but it was over. Over, over, over! His choice. She braked for a stoplight and waited impatiently, gloved fingers tapping on the steering wheel as a few brave souls bundled in scarves, boots and thick winter coats hurried along the snow-covered streets of Grand Hope. Barren trees lifted naked arms to a night sky where millions of snowflakes caught in the neon lights of the city continued to fall.

So what did you expect from him? A marriage proposal? Her wayward mind taunted as the light changed to green and she stepped on the accelerator.

The thought made her laugh without a grain of humor. Then minutes later, still lost in her own thoughts, she turned onto the street where she lived, and promised herself that she would get over Thorne McCafferty once and for all. She had her girls. She had her work. She had a life. Without Thorne. She didn't need him.

The SUV's wheels slid a bit as she pulled into the driveway but she managed to park in front of the garage. Hauling her briefcase and laptop computer with her, she dashed through the short drifts and climbed up the back porch. Stomping the snow from her boots and pulling off her gloves with her teeth, she opened the back door and heard squeals of delight.

"Mommy! Mommy! Come see." Two sets of feet pounded the floor as the girls raced into the kitchen.

Nicole was unzipping her coat, but leaned down to hug each of the twins. Yes, her life was full. She didn't need a man and certainly not Thorne McCafferty.

Patches hopped lithely onto the counter.

"The flowers. Bunches and bunches and bunches of flowers," Molly said, holding her arms as wide as she could.

"Flowers?" Nicole asked and noticed the fragrance of roses that seemed to permeate the air.

"Yeth." Mindy was pulling on one hand, dragging her to the living room. Molly gripped her other.

"You get down!" Nicole ordered the precocious feline as they passed the counter. The cat hopped to the floor as Nicole stepped into the living room and gasped. Jenny was standing near the fireplace and the grate was lit, several logs burning brightly, and all around the room, on every table, in the corners and on the floor, were dozens and dozens of roses. Red, white, pink, yellow—it didn't matter, bouquet after bouquet. "What in the world...?" she whispered.

"There's a card." Jenny pointed to a bouquet of three dozen white long-stemmed roses.

"Read it! Read it!" Both girls chimed.

With shaking fingers she opened the small white envelope. It read simply: "Marry me."

Tears burned behind her eyelids. "Do you know who sent these?" she asked.

Jenny smiled. "Don't you?"

Knees suddenly weak, Nicole dropped into a side chair. "Dear Lord..."

"What, Mommy? What?" Mindy asked, her little eyebrows knotting in concern.

"Thorne's in the hospital."

"What?" Jenny's smile fell away and haltingly Nicole told her about the plane crash.

"Oh, my God, well you've got to go back there. You've got to be with him."

"But the girls..."

"Don't worry about them. I can handle them." The twins' faces fell and Jenny added, "we'll have pizza delivered and make popcorn balls and...and a surprise for your mommy."

"But I don't want Mommy to leave," Mindy said.

"Baby!" Molly accused, pointing a tiny finger at her sister.

"Am not!"

"Shh...shh...no one's a baby."

Touched by the dazzling array of flowers, Nicole stared at the soft petals and long stems and her heart pounded with a love she so recently tried to deny.

"I—I do have to go back to the hospital," she said, "but I'll be back soon."

Mindy's face began to crumple. "Promise?"

Nicole kissed her daughter's forehead and stood on legs that threatened to give out again. She plucked one crimson rose from its vase and winked at her daughters. "Promise."

Through a veil of pain, he heard the door open and expected that it was the nurse bringing much needed medication.

"Thorne?"

Nicole's voice. His heart leaped, but he didn't move. Nor did she turn on the light as she walked to his bedside. Carefully she laid a long-stemmed rose on his chest. "I—I don't know what to say."

He didn't respond. Didn't move. In his semiconscious state a few hours ago, he'd heard her claims of loving him yet not wanting him, of saying it would never work out, so he'd thought she'd gotten the flowers and had rejected him. He hadn't been able to respond then, didn't know if he could now. He barely remembered the accident. There had been a problem, an engine had died and he'd been forced to land in a field, nearly made it when the plane had crashed into a copse of trees...he was lucky...

"I got the flowers. Dozens and dozens of them. You shouldn't have...oh Thorne," she whispered, dragging him back to the present, to Nicole. Beautiful, sexy Nicole. "I wish you could hear me. I want to explain...."

Here it comes again. She was going to repeat what

she'd said earlier. Without moving he braced himself for the worst.

"I was—am—overwhelmed." She cleared her throat and he felt her fingers find his. "I read the card."

He felt like an idiot. Why had he bared his soul to her? She didn't want him, she'd made that clear enough. He braced himself against the pain.

"And I wish I could make you hear me, that you'd understand just how much I love you. Marry you? Oh, Lord, if you only knew how much I wanted to do just that, but I saw your picture with that woman at the fund-raiser in Denver and I—I thought you weren't ready to settle down, that you never will be and so, I don't know what to do. If there was any chance that we could be together, you and I and the girls, believe me I'd—"

Despite the pain, he forced his hand to move. His head felt as if it might explode, but he grabbed her hand then, held on to it fiercely. The rose dropped to the floor.

"Oh! Dear God—"

"Marry me," he rasped, forcing the words through lips that felt cracked and swollen. Pain screamed through his body but he didn't care.

"But—what? Can you—"

"Marry me." He squeezed her fingers so tightly that she gasped again.

"You can hear me?"

He forced his eyes open, blinked against the fragile light that seemed to blind. "Nicole—would you please just answer?" Somehow he managed to focus on her face—God, it was a great face. "Will you marry me?"

"But what about the other woman, the one in the paper?"

"There is no other woman. Just you." He stared at her hard, willing her to believe him. "And there will always only be you in my life. I swear it."

He watched her swallow hard, bite her lip, fight the indecision.

"I will love you forever," he vowed and then the tears came, slowly at first and then more rapidly, falling from her gorgeous amber eyes. "Marry me, Nicole. Be my wife."

With her free hand, she dashed the tears away. "Yes," she whispered, her voice cracking. "Yes." He yanked hard, pulled her over him and when his lips found hers some of the pain disappeared and he knew that from this day forward he would gladly give up whatever possessions he had, that nothing else came close to the love he felt for her and he would cherish this woman until he gave up his very last breath.

"I love you, Doctor," he vowed as she lifted her head and laughed. "And this time, believe me, I'll never leave you and I'll never let you go."

"Oh, I bet you say that to all the women physicians," she teased, her eyes bright with tears as she picked up the rose and laid it next to him on the bed.

"Nope. Only one."

"Lucky me," she sniffed, leaning down and brushing her lips against his.

"No." Of this he was certain. "Lucky me."

Epilogue

"You're sure you want to live here?" Nicole asked, her gaze roving around the snow-covered acres as she and Thorne sat on the porch while the twins, in matching snowsuits, frolicked in the yard. The old dog, Harold, barked and joined them, acting like a pup, and cattle and horses dotted the landscape. Slade, dressed in a thick buckskin jacket, was walking near the barn, checking the pipes and watering troughs along with the stock.

It was beautiful here and Nicole's heart was full. Though Thorne's leg was casted, there was no keeping him down and they'd planned as soon as he was on his feet again to marry.

"I'll live here as long as Randi lets me."

Randi was the one worry. It had been nearly a month since her accident and she was still unconscious. Though Kurt Striker was still looking into the possibility of a hit-and-run driver forcing her off the road, he hadn't found any suspects and Thorne's plane crash was still under investigation. Was it foul play? Thorne hadn't thought so, or so he'd insisted, citing the fact that he should have had the plane checked out before flying off in the snowstorm. But he'd been anxious to return to Montana. "By the way," he said, "I have something for you."

"What's that?" she asked.

"Something to make our engagement official."

"Oh?" She lifted a wary eyebrow as he winced and dug into a front pocket of his jeans. Slowly he extracted a ring, a band of silver and gold.

"It was my father's, from his marriage to my Mom," he explained and Nicole was touched, her throat clogging suddenly as he slipped it onto her finger. "For some sentimental reason, the old man kept it even after the divorce and while he was married to Randi's mother. He gave it to me before he died and now...because of tradition, I guess, I want you to have it." His smile was crooked. "I think we'll have it sized to fit." The ring, an intricate band of gold and silver, was much too big for her finger but she clutched it tight, knowing that it meant so much to Thorne. That he would share it with her said more than words.

"It's beautiful."

"And special."

"Oh, Thorne, thank you," she whispered, then kissed him as he held her close and the old porch swing swayed.

"And you're special to me, Nicole, you and the girls."

She had trouble swallowing over the lump in her throat. Never in her wildest dreams had she thought she'd ever hear those words from Thorne McCafferty, the man who had so callously used her and then walked away.

As if he could read her thoughts, he placed a kiss upon her head. "I know I made a mistake with you and I've kicked myself a dozen times over, but I want to make it up to you, to the twins. I…I never thought I'd want to settle down, to have a family of my own to…" he struggled for a moment, looked across the snow-crusted fields "…to share my life here. On the Flying M. But I do. Because of you." His eyes found hers. "You're the one, Nicole. The only one."

She sighed against him and looked at the ring. God, she loved him. Blinking back tears of joy, she whispered, "I love you."

"Oh, you do, do you?" he said, a slow, sexy smile creeping from one side of his mouth to the other.

"Scout's honor," she said. His grin was infectious and she tossed a sassy smile back his way. "You don't believe me?"

"Maybe…"

"But maybe not?"

"You could prove it."

She laughed and rose to the bait. "And how would I do that?"

His eyes gleamed wickedly. "Oh, I can think of a dozen or two different ways."

"And I can think of a hundred."

He rose awkwardly to his feet and pulled her to

hers. "Then let's start, shall we? As my father would say, 'time's a wastin', and he did say he wanted some grandchildren."

"What about J.R. and the twins?"

"A start, lady, just a start."

"Slow down, Romeo," she said giggling.

"No way, lady. We've only got the rest of our lives."

She threw back her head and laughed huskily. "I do love you, Thorne McCafferty, but if anyone's going to have to do the proving it's you."

"All right." He swept her off her feet and she squealed.

"Thorne, don't! Your leg! For crying out loud, let me go! Put me down!"

He held her tight, his shoulder braced against the side of the house, his strong arms holding her close. "Never," he vowed, then kissed her hard. She closed her eyes, kissed him back and wondered if anyone had the right to feel this happy. As he lifted his head and stared into her eyes, he said again, "I will never let you go, Nicole. Never again."

And she believed him.

* * * * *

Look for Lisa Jackson's next book,
THE McCAFFERTYS: MATT,
available from Silhouette Special Edition
in mid-2001.

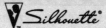

Don't miss this great offer to save on *New York Times* bestselling author **Linda Howard's** touching love story **SARAH'S CHILD,** a must have for any romance reader.

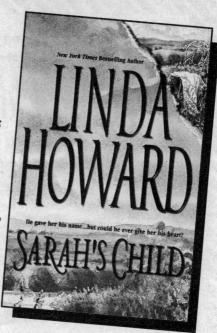

Available December 2000 wherever hardcovers are sold.

Don't miss this
great offer to save
on *New York Times*
bestselling author
Linda Howard's
touching love story

SARAH'S CHILD,
a must have for any
romance reader.

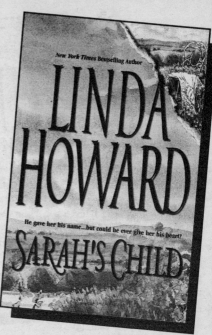

Available December 2000 wherever hardcovers are sold.

Silhouette® —

where love comes alive—online...

eHARLEQUIN.com

your romantic
books

♥ **Shop online!** Visit Shop eHarlequin and discover a wide selection of new releases and classic favorites at great discounted prices.

♥ **Read** our daily and weekly Internet exclusive serials, and participate in our interactive novel in the reading room.

♥ **Ever dreamed of being a writer?** Enter your chapter for a chance to become a featured author in our Writing Round Robin novel.

• • • • • •

your romantic
life

♥ **Check out** our feature articles on dating, flirting and other important romance topics and get your daily love dose with tips on how to keep the romance alive every day.

• • • • • •

your
community

♥ **Have a Heart-to-Heart** with other members about the latest books and meet your favorite authors.

♥ **Discuss** your romantic dilemma in the Tales from the Heart message board.

your romantic
escapes

♥ **Learn** what the stars have in store for you with our daily Passionscopes and weekly Erotiscopes.

♥ **Get the latest scoop** on your favorite royals in Royal Romance.

Silhouette®

COMING NEXT MONTH

#1369 THE TYCOON'S INSTANT DAUGHTER—
Christine Rimmer
The Stockwells of Texas
Accomplished playboy Cord Stockwell managed to juggle the
family business, his newfound infant daughter and her irritating—
yet irresistible—social worker, Miss Hannah Miller. But when
Cord hired Hannah as the baby's nanny, could he keep the
relationship strictly business?

#1370 UNEXPECTEDLY EXPECTING!—Susan Mallery
Lone Star Canyon
Nora Darby had sworn off men yet still dreamt of motherhood.
Big-city doctor Stephen Remington moved to Lone Star Canyon
with hopes of mending his shattered heart. A night of passion and
an unexpected pregnancy may have been just what these love-
wary souls needed....

#1371 JUDGING JUSTINE—Penny Richards
Rumor Has It...
A scandalous past forced Justine Sutton to leave home and
make a fresh start in Nashville. When long-ago love Wes Grayson
reappeared in Justine's life, she feared the past would reclaim her.
Had she finally discovered that love could heal all?

#1372 PRETEND ENGAGEMENT—Tracy Sinclair
American tourist Jillian Colby fled from the altar when she found
out her Italian fiancé was a fraud. Fortunately for her, she ran into
Gianni di Destino, Duke of Venetia, who helped Jillian ward off
her nosy family with a pretend engagement...that could turn out to
be the real thing!

#1373 THE NOT-SO-SECRET BABY—Diana Whitney
Stork Express
Susan Mitchell, a beautiful teacher, found out that she was
pregnant after she spent a spontaneous night of passion with
widowed rancher Jarod Bodine. Jarod never expected to see Susan
again and was shocked when she showed up several weeks later to
tutor his eight-year-old son. But Susan had returned to teach a
very important lesson...fatherhood.

#1374 BELOVED BACHELOR DAD—Crystal Green
In an attempt to save a student's future, teacher Nora Murray
confronted single father Ray Brody about his rebellious son's
behavior. While Ray's son Trent secretly played matchmaker, the
couple found it hard to deny their sizzling attraction. Could they
beat the odds and come together as a family?

SPECIAL EDITION